9.95
B+T

The Himalayan Kingdoms

The Himalayan Kingdoms

Nepal, Bhutan and Sikkim

Bob Gibbons
and
Bob Ashford

HIPPOCRENE
BOOKS, INC.

New York, N.Y.

Paperback edition published in the USA in 1987 by
Hippocrene Books, Inc.
171 Madison Ave.
New York, N.Y. 10016

ISBN 0–87052–464–X

Contents

List of Illustrations

Maps

Acknowledgment

We would like to extend our thanks to the following: Liz Gibbons for the maps of Nepal, Peregrine Expeditions of Melbourne for the map of Sikkim, and Patrick Leeson for the map of the general area and for Bhutan. Pat Robinson kindly supplied the photograph showing Bob Gibbons and friend crossing the Langtang Khola while on the Durham University Himalayan expedition.

Our particular thanks go to Liz and Nos for their help and forbearance throughout.

The photographs were supplied as follows: Bob Gibbons for photos 1, 2, 3, 4, 6, 13, 17, 18, 21, 22, 23, 24, 25 and 26. Bob Ashford took photos 7, 8, 9, 10, 11, 12, 14, 15, 16, 19, 20, 27, 28, 29, 30, 31, 32, 33, 34, 35, 36, 37, 38, 39. Pat Robinson took photo 5.

1. Introduction to the Himalayan Kingdoms

Nepal. Bhutan. Sikkim. The names themselves have a magical ring, conjuring up visions of fertile shangri-las amongst snow-capped mountains, lost in the Middle Ages. In a sense, this is not far from the truth, especially for Bhutan, but there have been enormous changes in all these countries within the last thirty years as they have entered the twentieth century in their different ways. Bhutan and Nepal are genuine mountain kingdoms, Bhutan with its Buddhist monarchy and Nepal with its Hindu monarchy (the only one in the world), but Sikkim, unfortunately, is no longer either. Since 1975 it has been the twenty-second state of the Republic of India, and is thus more correctly described as a Hindu state (though it was a Buddhist kingdom), but it has retained its old boundaries and much of the culture of the old Kingdom of Sikkim, so has been included here as if it were still so. It remains to be seen how Indian influence will alter this traditional way of life, though the signs are not hopeful.

It is intriguing that these southern slopes of the Himalayas should have spawned so many small independent kingdoms. They are sandwiched between two of the largest and most populous nations on Earth – India and China – yet they have remained largely separate and distinct. The answer lies partly in physical and partly in political terms. Mountains have a tendency to support small kingdoms anyway, because of the difficulties of access, communication and warfare. But the Himalayas are more than just ordinary mountains. They are the highest mountains on Earth, stretching in an unbroken chain for thousands of miles, forming an almost impenetrable wall. More than that, they form the barrier between two worlds, with the dry, barren, high altitude Tibetan and Mongolian world to the north, and the low-lying tropical fertile monsoonal Hindu world to the south. The two are so totally different to each other that it is almost impossible to imagine them meeting.

How totally different it would be if the Himalayas were not there.

When the British ruled in India, up until 1947, rather than take their borders right up to those of major unfriendly powers, they sometimes found it expedient to support buffer states between themselves and their larger neighbours. The existing kingdoms of the Himalayas probably suited their purpose admirably, and while it is clear that they could have annexed all three without enormous difficulty, they preferred not to, and their role became one of support, letting the buffer states absorb minor disputes, only stepping in themselves when really necessary.

But the British have gone, the Chinese are in Tibet in force and have built roads to the north side of the Himalayas, and policies have begun to change. Each of the major powers, now China and India, has sought to influence the buffer states increasingly. Sikkim has now gone as an independent state, and we can only hope that Nepal and Bhutan are strong enough to remain independent.

These three areas share so many physical and cultural features in common that it is hardly surprising that relations between them have been generally cordial. There have been times, however, when relations did become strained, and war has even broken out. During the late eighteenth century, Nepal was trying to expand its borders under the Gorkha Shah kings, and Sikkim was one of the directions in which they turned, such that at one time they came to occupy much of western Sikkim. At the same time, Bhutan supported Sikkim against Nepal, so that relations between Nepal and Bhutan became severely strained, though Sikkim has always acted as a buffer between these two countries. Sikkim has also suffered incursions from the Bhutanese side in the past. Although relationships with Tibet or India have dominated the foreign policies of all three countries, they have continued to have relations with each other, with Nepal always the dominant partner. Sikkim, as the smallest country in Central Asia, both physically and numerically, has been considerably affected by her neighbours, and largely dependent on their territorial aspirations. The Nepalese people have frequently migrated into both Sikkim and Bhutan, and their influence on the cultures of both countries has been strong and lasting.

Today, relationships between Bhutan and Nepal are as good as they have ever been. The late king of Bhutan, Jigme Dorji Wangchuck, attended the coronation of the late King Mahendra in Kathmandu in 1956, and Bhutan mourned for three days when

Mahendra died, as did Nepal when Jigme Dorji died. The corona-tion of the present king of Bhutan, Jigme Singe Wangchuck, was attended by a Nepalese delegation headed by Prince Dhirendra, and similarly King Birendra's coronation in Nepal was attended by a Bhutanese delegation. So, the two countries have developed close ties, at all levels, and they share a strong policy of peace, friendship and non-alignment.

For us, the western visitor, all three countries provide an unrivalled opportunity to sample a way of life and a landscape that has more in common with medieval times then the present day. All three countries have opened their doors in the last twenty years, and great changes have been made. Yet, away from the main towns and centres or along the few main roads, the countries remain essentially unspoilt, with no roads, no vehicles and a strong community and religious spirit. The differences between the centres of population and the hill villages, perhaps six days' walk from a road, are becoming increasingly sharp as the towns develop and expand, particularly in Nepal. Many of the towns are still beautiful places, despite their overlay of modern trappings, but we have tried throughout this book to tempt people away from the modern expressions of each country into the still roadless hills and valleys.

As has just been mentioned, one of the attributes that these three countries share is that of difficult access. There are few roads, no railways, and only scattered airstrips for STOL (short take-off and landing) planes. Yet everywhere in this region, from the highest passes to the tropical jungles, there are foot trails, and throughout this book we have tried to emphasize that the best way to see and feel the Himalayas is on foot, using the way that the vast majority of the local people uses. Although it is worth every effort expended, it is not a matter to be undertaken lightly, and this chapter is intended as an outline guide to the considerations required to get the best from a 'trek' in the Himalayas. If you are visiting the area, don't miss the chance of a trek if you can possibly help it.

Before the trip it is wise to embark on a programme of weekend walking well in advance, not only to get fitter and identify any physical problems, but also to get accustomed to the boots or shoes that you will be using. Comfortable clothing and equipment can make all the difference to one's enjoyment of a trek, but it is essential to test everything thoroughly first. A mountain walk anywhere in rough country will be comparable for this purpose, the longer the better.

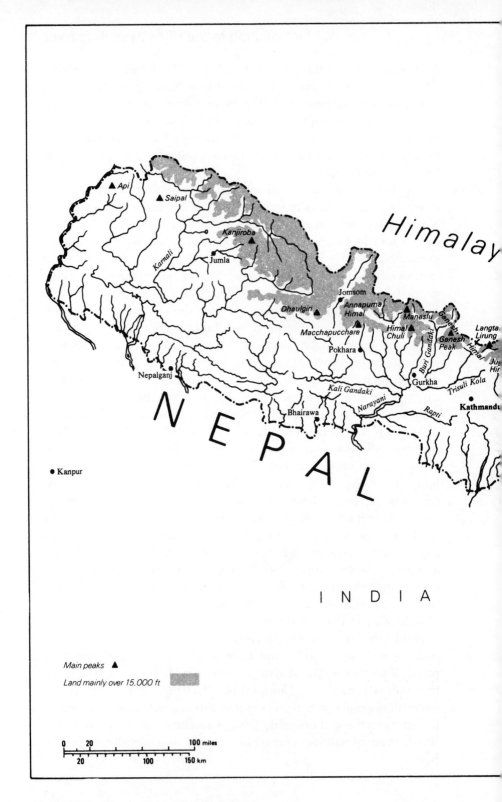

Nepal, Sikkim, Bhutan and adjoining countries

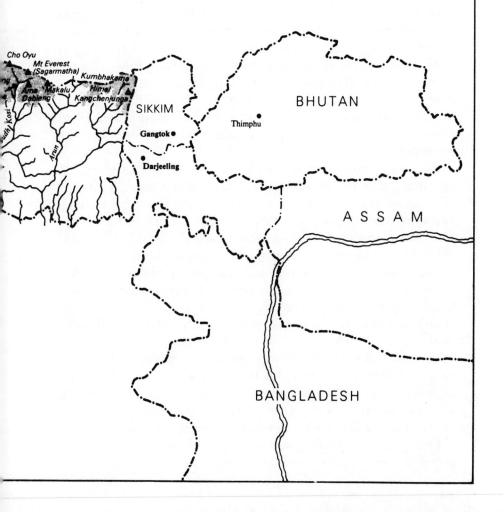

C H I N A
(T I B E T)

Lhasa ●

ange

Cho Oyu
Mt Everest
(Sagarmatha)
Kumbhakarna
Ama
Dablang
Makalu
Himal
Kangchenjunga

SIKKIM

Thimphu

BHUTAN

Gangtok ●

Darjeeling

Arun

Dudh Kosi

ASSAM

BANGLADESH

It is essential to have a thorough medical check-up before leaving, and to take the doctor's advice on whether to go or not. Poor fillings in teeth can become particularly painful at high altitudes, so a complete dental check-up is also advisable. Some preliminary injections are essential, and others are worthwhile, as advised by your doctor. It is worth taking a small first-aid kit.

Knowing when to go is an important consideration. In brief, October to December is perfect trekking weather, with clear blue skies and fabulous views in the sparkling post-monsoon weather. Winter, December to March, is cold and clear, with snow on the high slopes – a beautiful season, but with really low night temperatures at high altitudes, and many passes blocked by snow. Spring, from March to May, is the time for rhododendrons, and all forms of wildlife, and the weather is generally good. The dust begins to build up as the weather gets hotter and the plains get drier, and there may be frequent thunderstorms around the mountains in May. Summer, from June to September, is predominantly monsoon time, and unfortunately it really does rain, though not quite every day. It is the time to see the alpine pastures in full flower, and the occasional sunny moments are magical, but it is a time of frequent rain and mist, floods, broken bridges, and – perhaps worst of all – leeches! Most people avoid summer for travelling in the mountains, though it does have its advantages.

There are three ways in which one can organize a trek: self-contained, carrying all you need for yourself; organizing your own trip, but using porters and/or Sherpas; or going through a trekking agency or tour company to get a fully organized and inclusive trip. Each has its merits. Travelling self-contained is cheap, flexible and enjoyable, as long as you do not mind the constant burden of a heavy rucksack even on the steepest hills and at the highest altitudes. Travelling with a few porters, and perhaps a Sherpa whom you have hired yourself or through an agency, can be a great deal more luxurious than carrying your own gear and catering for yourself, and it is almost as flexible, though it is more expensive and you may experience problems with porters who are not 'regulars' for a good agency. Porters simply carry loads, up to about 65 pounds weight, whereas Sherpas lead, guide, organize porters, the purchase of food, selection and organization of campsites and so on, and a good Sherpa or Sirdar (head Sherpa) is more than worth the wages you pay him.

Finally one can go in for group travel, by booking a ready-made trip through an agency or tour company, as many people do. This need not work out more expensive than going it alone with your own staff, as many of the costs are shared, and you have the advantage of pleasant evenings around the fire or in the local tea house with your companions. It is less flexible than travelling alone – though generally tour companies appreciate what people want to do and how long they will take – and one may also experience less contact with local people, but this is undoubtedly the easiest way to travel in the Himalayas. In Bhutan and Sikkim it is virtually the only way, as individual travel is not generally permitted yet.

As to accommodation, a few years ago there was hardly anywhere to stay while walking in the Himalayas, except in a few traditionally hospitable areas. But now, in Nepal, there are lodges of some sort in almost every village, along all the better known routes, right up to the limits of habitation. These are normally simple wooden or stone buildings, with sleeping areas often communal, and cheap basic food available – usually rice, dhal (lentils), eggs, and perhaps some fruit or vegetables. Generally they are remarkably cheap – though prices have risen dramatically – but you will find that food prices increase at the higher altitudes as everything has to be brought into these areas. Agriculture at high altitudes is a precarious and unproductive business, and there is little surplus for sale to visitors, and anyway most visitors prefer the less basic food. In Sikkim and Bhutan these lodges do not generally exist, though there are a few mountaineering huts in Sikkim. It is also possible to sleep in local people's houses in the friendlier villages, though one can be less certain of the conditions, and this frequently leads to a week of scratching afterwards! There are also a few much more luxurious hotels in the mountains, in Nepal only, usually adjacent to an airstrip or major centre. These are much more expensive, but provide facilities almost to normal hotel standards, with more varied food flown in from Kathmandu. They are too infrequent to be of much use to the walker, though perhaps worthwhile if you need an occasional rejuvenation and a hot bath. . . . Tents can of course be carried, and there is no shortage of places to pitch a tent.

The Himalayas must be one of the most rewarding places in the world for photography, and almost everyone can bring back some impressive shots. It's well worth giving some thought to your equipment and film in advance, though, because it is easy to go inadequately prepared and be disappointed with the results.

Almost any type of camera will take good pictures, and there is something to be said for all types. If you intend only to take general pictures and shots of people, buildings, etc., then it is probably easiest to take a 'compact' 35mm camera which you can carry with you everywhere, and which should produce excellent quality results. If, however, you intend to take a wider range of more difficult shots – natural history, candids, special effects, close-ups – then you will be far better served by a single lens reflex (SLR) with the facility to change lenses, add close-up equipment and so on. The possibilities of such a camera system are endless, and one can cope with almost any situation. If you have a camera with interchangeable lenses, you will find some additional lenses useful: a wide angle, e.g. 28mm, is useful for interiors, buildings, and occasionally views; a short telephoto, e.g. 135mm, or 70 to 150mm zoom, is particularly useful for views, portraits, candid shots, etc., and is probably the most useful additional lens to have. Those interested in natural history photography will find a macro lens invaluable, e.g. 90mm or 50mm, and a 50mm macro can take the place of a standard lens. Longer telephotos are useful for more specialized applications – wildlife, mountain tops and so on – but they are heavy and bulky, and you need to be sure you will make use of it.

An electronic flashgun or two can be very useful for interiors, evening shots, fill-in flash in harsh sunlight, and for really sharp close-ups. Be sure to take enough spare batteries. One of the most useful accessories for the Himalayan photographer is a polarizing filter. These cut out polarized light, and the net effect on a suitable landscape of mountain and sky is dramatic. Skies become bluer, and clouds become whiter, and the whole scene takes on a greater clarity of form and detail. They are also invaluable for removing unwanted reflections, e.g. from water or windows. If you do not carry a polarizing filter, it is invaluable to have at least an ultra-violet (UV) or skylight filter which can be left on the lens as protection, and improves distant views or shade shots. Yellow and orange filters are particularly useful for black and white photography.

A 2x teleconverter can be useful, as space and weight are at a premium. These double the focal length of any lens which they are used with, though at the same time they cause a loss of two-stops exposure, and some loss of quality.

If you take much equipment, a compact and robust carrying bag is a boon to keep it all together and under your control, as well as protecting it from the elements.

Finally, film. Take as much as you possibly can – it is not readily available in these areas, and you will probably use more than you thought you would. Unless going in the monsoon, it is wise to take a relatively slow, good quality film, such as Kodachrome 25, together with a small amount of faster film for occasional use, unless you have specialized requirements.

Regarding photography itself, a few pointers may help to improve the results, and reduce the number consigned to the wastepaper basket. Always carry a camera set ready for action, preferably with the exposure set ready for the conditions – many shots give only a fleeting chance of success. Very early morning in the mountains, from about 5.00 a.m. onwards, is an excellent time to be taking photographs as the peaks catch the early sun. A little later on is a good time for wildlife, general views, frost shots, mist and so on, before the heat of the day, and before everyone else is up and about. Most people do not mind being photographed, though women and Hindus need treating with more caution. It is essential to respect people's wishes. Rhododendrons make the perfect counterbalance to a mountain snow scene. A short telephoto can bring the two elements closer together, and a small aperture should be used to bring both into focus. Tall buildings are best photographed from a distance, using a short telephoto. If you need to use a wide angle, where you cannot get back from the buildings, try to ensure that the camera is precisely upright or the picture will appear distorted. Snow scenes can be difficult. Most modern cameras expose for snow quite accurately if the meter is followed, but where there are people, buildings, or other dark objects, you will need to give more exposure than indicated to ensure that they are correctly exposed. They will appear too dark if the snow is exposed for. People can enhance some landscapes, and it is often worth going ahead of a group of travellers and waiting until they are exactly where you want in order to give just the right picture.

Finding your way needs some careful thought in advance. If you are travelling without a guide, it is perfectly possible to get lost. Most trek trails are main trails, but the way is by no means always clear, and there are very few signs to go by. There are no really good maps available generally, though there are a number of reasonable trekking maps for the main areas of Nepal, which show the trails, the main villages and physical features, though they may not be totally accurate and are not always detailed enough. There are reasonable general maps available for Sikkim, showing villages and physical features, but not indicating trekking routes. Bhutan has no readily available adequate maps. In Nepal, it is best to combine the maps with one of the guide books to treks which describe the route and note any difficulties. These are readily available in Kathmandu. If you have neither map, book nor guide, it will be useful to have a note of the main towns and villages that you hope to pass through on your route. Most villagers if faced with the question 'To Everest?' accompanied by a pointing finger, will either be nonplussed or will say 'yes' to whichever trail you point out.

The realities of altitude problems cannot be overstressed. If you are travelling with a group, the problems should be minimized because the leader will be constantly alert to your problems; but if you are alone or in a small group, never carry on gaining height if you feel light-headed, sick or have a headache. If matters get worse, it is essential to lose height. At high altitudes, it is essential to have periods of acclimatization between large gains in height. Altitude sickness is unpredictable in its effects and choice of victims, and the fit and healthy are by no means immune. The dangers are very real, and travellers have died through ignoring the warning signs. Although a supply of diuretics (e.g. Lasex) and Vitamin E are helpful in reducing the severity of the problem, there is only one specific remedy for altitude problems – to lose height rapidly.

2. Nepal: Geography, Climate and Travel

In 1951, a major event in the history of tourism occurred. The mountainous Kingdom of Nepal ended its long period of self-imposed isolation from the outside world and opened its boundaries to visitors from all countries.

The reasons behind this change, and the results of plunging from medieval feudalism to twentieth-century madness are discussed later. The relevant fact here is that it is now possible to visit this fascinating Himalayan country which still retains so much of its original charm and way of life, set amongst some of the most impressive mountain scenery in the world. Now, over twenty-five years after the country first opened its doors, an estimated quarter of a million people per year visit Nepal, increasing every year. They come for a variety of reasons, but foremost amongst the attractions are, of course, the Himalayas with their beautiful and often unbelievable scenery, their isolated monasteries and undisturbed way of life, and their profusion of wildlife and flowers. Although there are no roads leading into the mountains, excepting the Chinese road to Lhasa which crosses a low pass, many towns lie close below the mountains, and the vast network of footpaths allow almost anyone to reach the highest valleys. Because there were no roads, railways, telephones or airstrips at all until recently, walking has always been the traditional method of travel, as it still is in 95 per cent of the country, and the visiting walker is therefore well catered for. Although it is now possible to fly within a few miles of Mount Everest, or take a helicopter and land for an hour in a remote valley, there is no doubt that the best way by far to see the country is to get out and walk. Our aim throughout this section is to show that the deeper that one looks in Nepal, the more rewarding and fascinating it becomes.

Religion is a part of the daily life of most of the Nepalese people, and has been for thousands of years. Various religions, particularly

Hinduism and Buddhism, cohabit and mix peacefully, and the result is a profusion of beautiful temples, monasteries and shrines. Largely because of the industry of the indigenous Newar people, the Kathmandu valley has the most concentrated assemblage of temples in Nepal, and Kathmandu itself is said to have more temples per square mile than any other city in the world. The adjacent old towns of Patan (Lalitpur) and Bhadgaon (Bhaktapur) are equally rich, with less new building to obscure the old. For many visitors, this display of history and religion is the prime reason for coming to Nepal, and for any visitor the splendours of the 2000 year old Swyambunath Buddhist temple, or the rigidly Hindu Pashupatinath, are not to be missed. Throughout the year, there are constant religious festivals for one god or another. The Nepalese love any chance of a festival, and, because there are so many gods to worship, there is a regular flow of colourful ceremonies in one part of the valley or another. Collections of noisy weddings occur at auspicious times, determined by the stars, and jazz bands march the streets playing a mixture of Indian pop songs and traditional tunes to proclaim the happy events. While we were there one March, several bands marched through the streets for weeks on end, vying with – and occasionally meeting – each other, as this was one of the most auspicious times for many years for weddings, preceding a long inauspicious period.

Sadly, many of the visitors who come to visit Nepal do not stay for more than a few days, often as part of a longer Asian or Indian tour, and they thus miss much of the interest of the country.

One of the greatest attractions for the less casual visitor is the wealth of natural history. The country's position in the sub-tropics, coupled with its altitude range from 200 to over 29,000 feet has allowed the development of almost all vegetation types from near-tropical to arctic or alpine. Associated with this is an incredible variety of animals, birds, reptiles, insects and plants. For instance, nearly 10 per cent (just over 800) of the world's bird species are recorded from Nepal, a country little larger than England. It is now possible to take a most unusual holiday in the Chitwan National Park, specifically to watch wildlife. This area of the Terai still supports many of the original Indian sub-continent mammals, such as tiger, and the one-horned rhinoceros, and an East African style operation allows the visitor to view much of the teeming wildlife at close range from elephant back or carefully sited hides. Even here, the Himalayas show their presence, and although over fifty miles away, they almost hang over the park, 20,000 feet above it.

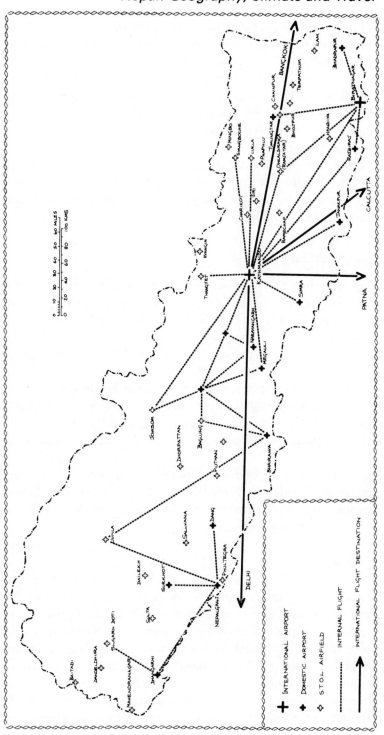

Nepal's airstrips and flight paths

One of the perennial attractions of Nepal, and one which started before the present influx of visitors, is of course mountaineering. An almost unbroken line of mountains, over 500 miles long, with ten major peaks over 26,000 feet, and more than 200 peaks over 20,000 feet, cannot fail to attract mountaineers; in spite of rapidly increasing costs, there are still large numbers of climbing expeditions every year to Nepal, and trips to the major peaks are booked up for years to come.

Lastly among Nepal's attractions may be mentioned the way of life. People, mainly young people from the richer west, come to Nepal and often stay for a while, in order to sample a completely different outlook on life.

Geographical Features

The Kingdom of Nepal forms an oblique rectangle, roughly 500 miles long and 120 miles deep, covering an area of 54,000 square miles, about half that of the British Isles. Its latitude is almost sub-tropical, more or less equal to those of Mexico, Cairo or Hong Kong. The greater part of the country lies on the southern slope of the Himalayas, extending down from the highest peaks to the upper edge of the Ganges plain, where the country borders with India. For much of its length the country's northern border, with China, runs along the ridge of peaks, though a wedge of the trans-Himalayan area is within the boundaries to the northwest. To the east lies Sikkim.

The country may be divided into five zones, which are reasonably clearly distinguished. From the south, these are: the Terai, the Siwalik zone, the Mahabharat Lekh, the midlands or Pahar zone, and lastly the Himalayas.

The Terai

This is probably the most clearly defined of the zones, extending north from the Indian border to where the first foothills rise sharply out of the plains, and consisting of a flat strip, the upper part of the great Ganges plain. It runs for the whole length of Nepal, nowhere more than thirty miles in width and occasionally disappearing altogether where the Indian border reaches north to the foot of the Siwalik hills. Once it was an undisturbed, uninhabited malarial paradise, shunned by the hill people. It is still the haunt of vast numbers of mosquitoes to whose voracious appetites we can personally testify, but since the decline of malaria in recent years, more and more people have come to settle there because of the fertile soil and sub-tropical climate. The indigenous or long-established peoples of the area are the Tharus, a fascinating race who exhibit apparent partial resistance to the dreaded malaria, and who live in close harmony with their environment, so that until recently dense forest full of wildlife extended over the whole region. With the influx of settlers, this quickly disappeared in many areas.

The character of the Terai is best seen by flying over it: scarred river valleys up to a mile wide intersect a patchwork of forest and cleared areas. For much of the year, these river valleys are almost dry, while for a few short months in summer they are flooded from bank to bank with a restless silted torrent, changing course from year to year on the way to the Ganges. The problems of communication under such conditions are enormous, and few roads cross the Terai from east to west. The houses of many of the people stand upon poles or stilts as a protection against floods or wild animals.

The Siwalik Zone

The Siwalik hills, or Churia range, form the outermost ramparts of the great Himalayas, rising directly from the Ganges plain to reach a height of about 4000 feet. The area is almost completely uninhabited, for the slopes are steep, and during much of the year the land is without water. To the north of these outliers run the great transverse duns or wide valleys, such as the Rapti Dun, which in places separate the Siwalik range from the Mahabharat Lekh.

The Mahabharat Lekh

In any country but Nepal, the Mahabharat Lekh would be the prime feature of the landscape. It is a range of hills, whose steep summits rise to over 9000 feet, clad with deciduous forest, forming a protective barrier between the great plains and the fertile midlands. The lower slopes of the hills are inhabited by people of many races, albeit sparsely; Thamang and Chepang villages cling precariously to the hillsides, amongst an incredible network of endless terraces. As one climbs up the slopes, the villages diminish, and most of the summits are still covered with dense virgin forest. It is an intriguing fact that almost all the waters of Nepal, and some from Tibet, pass through three gorges in the Mahabharat Lekh. All the rivers join together into three main rivers which have forced their way through the hills with their combined power. In places, there are passes as low as 700 feet, and several roads and trade trails cross the range. The whole area has a particular dramatic beauty of its own, yet is rarely visited by the tourist, for whom the sight of the Himalayas is an irresistible lure.

The Nepal Midlands

This central strip of Nepal, sometimes known as the Pahar zone, is by far the most densely populated part of the country, and one of the most intriguing. The Kathmandu and Pokhara valleys both lie within this area, and it is here that a high proportion of the population lives. The midlands, although not always clearly defined, form a sort of protected zone, bounded to the south by the Mahabharat Lekh and to the north by the Himalayas. In the past, it has been protected from invaders, and it is spared the cold winds from Tibet and the dusty heat of India. It occupies, therefore, a uniquely favourable position; the climate is pleasant, the slopes relatively gentle, and the soil usually fertile, so that crops of every type can be grown here. The altitude ranges from 2000 to 7000 feet, and the breadth of the zone is between thirty and sixty miles. The rich and fertile Kathmandu valley lies at an altitude of about 4000 feet, and it is no surprise that over half a million people live here within a 200 square mile area. The whole valley is the former bed of a lake, where the soil is particularly fertile, and as a consequence a vast variety of crops are grown here to satisfy both local needs and those of the increasingly sophisticated tourists. Three rivers cross the valley: the Bagmati, the Manahara and the Vishnumati, all of which eventually unite to flow out of the valley to the southeast, after breaching a low range of limestone hills by a dramatic gorge at Chobar. They flow southwards to eventually join the great Ganges, and are therefore all held in particular esteem by the Hindus.

The highest point around the Kathmandu valley is Pulchowk, 9000 feet above Godavari at the southwestern corner of the valley. The hill still retains a cover of exceptionally beautiful forest, and the view from the top, by the radio mast, is superb. Away to the south lie range after range of lower hills, stretching away to the dusty Indian plains, while to the north the snowy peaks rise up over the Kathmandu valley. It is well worth the effort of getting there.

Just over 120 miles to the west of Kathmandu is the beautiful valley of Pokhara. Although over 2000 feet lower than the Kathmandu valley, it is closer to the mountains, and the views are spectacular. Most of the area is limestone, and is seamed with caves into which whole rivers occasionally disappear.

The Himalayas

Arising sharply out of the midlands, sometimes with gradually increasing foothills and sometimes more abruptly, are the great Himalayas. Not only are the highest peaks in the world included in the Nepalese Himalayas, but so are many other peaks over 25,000 feet. They tower over the rest of the country, dwarfing man and nature alike. At times, it is difficult to appreciate just how high the Himalayas are, they are so far removed from most people's normal experience. They appear like clouds, higher than mountains could possibly be, so that one automatically assumes that they are smaller mountains when one is at closer range. Their true size is best appreciated, perhaps, from Pokhara, where the peaks of Annapurna, Macchapucchare and others rise sharply from the low-lying plain. The 23,000 foot summit of Macchapucchare is only fifteen miles from the centre of Pokhara, at 2500 feet. When trekking in the higher valleys, peaks which are, perhaps, 15,000 feet above may be only a mile away, though it is often difficult to comprehend, because the clear air and sheer unlikeliness of it all makes them seem smaller.

Between Annapurna and Dhaulgiri runs the Kali Gandaki river valley, at this point said to be the deepest valley in the world. The horizontal distance between these two peaks, both over 26,000 feet, is only a little over twenty miles, while the valley bottom at Dana is at 3800 feet. Now, after several years' closure, this incredible valley is again open to tourists, though trekkers to Ghorepani have long been able to view it from Poon hill.

The southern slopes of the Himalayas are well populated, especially in central and eastern Nepal, with numerous small villages amongst huge hillsides of terraces. Higher up, the number of villages decreases with the increased difficulties for agriculture, and the increased acreage required for pasturing animals (mainly yaks and yak-cattle hybrids at higher altitudes). The population in the very highest valleys is thought to be decreasing, as some younger people leave to work in the towns, though the trend is somewhat balanced by Tibetan settlers of recent origin. The highest permanent settlements occur at about 14,000 feet, varying according to latitude, and often the population is largely Tibetan, or mixed Tibetan and Thamang, as at Kyangin (13,500 feet), the highest village in the Langtang valley and one of the highest in Nepal.

Behind the main chain of peaks lie further valleys and peaks, known as the inner Himalayas. The valleys are often wide and flat, partly through glaciation, and partly through the softer nature of the rock here. Beyond the inner Himalayas again lie the Tibetan marginal mountains on the rim of the Tibetan plateau. Some of these, including the great Gosainthan (Shisha Pangma), 26,000 feet high, lie out of Nepal, and collectively they form the watershed between the Ganges to the south and the Tsangpo (Brahmaputra) in Chinese Tibet. It is this strange fact that gives rise to the deep valleys, such as the Arun and the Kali Gandaki, cutting through the main Himalayan range, which is not in itself the principal watershed. The Himalayas are possibly the newest mountains in the world, and their rapid upheaval across the path of existing rivers has caused these rivers to either divert around the range, or to find a way through.

The Climate

Nepal's weather is, generally speaking, predictable and pleasant. But, since the country lies in the monsoon belt of southern Asia, for four months of the year it receives the moisture-laden winds from the southeast, bringing with them the life-giving summer rain. From June to September, throughout most of the country, over 100 inches of rain may fall, while for the remaining two-thirds of the year there is virtual drought in many areas, broken only by a few thunderstorms, or snow in the mountains. Outside the monsoon period, the skies are often clear, and the sun usually shines.

For the visitor, the best time of year is autumn (October and November), when the sky is an incredible clear blue, the mountains stand sparkling white seemingly only a few miles away, the fields are green, and everywhere is clear and clean. Four months of heavy rain has a considerable effect on the appearance of the country. At this time of year it is, in general, neither too hot in the lowlands nor too cold in the mountains, though there is considerable variation between the two. Probably the most reliable month overall for sunny weather is November. We have trekked to Everest, Langtang, and many other areas during November, to heights over 18,000 feet, and no rain has fallen during the whole period, while the sun has shone every day except for a few days of mist in the Dudh Kosi. It is a remarkable time for viewing the country.

Towards the end of November it begins to get very cold at night in the highlands, while December, though still dry, is colder still. In Kathmandu, the daytime is very pleasant, the evenings cool, and the nights cold, though frost is virtually unknown there. In the New Year, a period begins during which much snow falls in the mountains and higher hills. The peaks which had turned brown or grey through the dry autumn turn white again, and snow may fall down to altitudes as low as 5000 to 6000 feet, though it is virtually unknown in Kathmandu. This snow continues as scattered showers in the highlands through to March, or even April, though there is plenty of sunshine during this period, increasing as spring approaches.

March–April is another excellent time to visit Nepal. The weather is good, though it will begin to get very warm later, and spring is beginning. Crops are sprouting, numerous shrubs begin to flower in the forests, and blue irises and primulas start to appear in the winter-browned mountain pastures. Hillsides are ablaze with red and pink rhododendrons, and the summer birds and butterflies make their first appearance. It is an exciting time to be in Nepal, though the great drawback is the dust. This spreads up in clouds from the dry, hot plains of India, and gradually the views become more and more hazy as the dust moves up the hills with the advancing spring. It is not a thick choking dust, but rather a dull haze obscuring the distant views, while above 10,000 feet it is completely absent. Once in the high valleys at this time of year, the views are as good as ever except that, to the south, the haze stretches away to the distant horizon.

In May, the air becomes dull and heavy in the lowlands, and the first summer thunderstorms start to build up. At first, they come only in the evenings, but gradually their frequency increases until, in some areas, there may be almost continual rain or cloud well in advance of the true monsoon. In other areas, there may be quite long dry periods between the showers still, though everywhere gets hotter all the time. On the southern slopes of Annapurna, and around Pokhara, one of the wettest areas of Nepal, May can be a period of almost continual rain or hail, broken only by odd days of sunshine, while in Kathmandu at the same time, many of the days may be fine with only evening thunderstorms.

In the middle of June the monsoon arrives. Its coming is eagerly awaited, for the fields are parched, the rivers are nearly dry, and the crops are waiting. Although it does not have quite the significance of the arrival of the monsoon in India, where the heat and drought are considerably greater, it is, nevertheless, a vital annual event. The start of the monsoon is marked by a change in the wind from southwesterly to southeasterly, though in the first few weeks it may give way to the southwesterly thunderstorms, again for short periods. Gradually the constant moist southeasterly air stream, blowing up from the Bay of Bengal, takes over and a new monsoon begins in earnest. Although so much rain does fall in summer, there is by no means continuous cloud. Most days start clear for a short period before the clouds build up and the rain falls, and in Kathmandu much of the rain falls at night. Those who are hardy enough to be in the mountains at this time of year may occasionally be rewarded with superb mountain views, though these may often last only for a few minutes, or even seconds, and for much of the rest of the time the traveller moves in mist and rain or drizzle.

In some years, there may be quite long periods, as long as two weeks, when there is no rain at all, while in other years rain may fall almost continuously through the monsoon period. Similarly, the time when the monsoon starts and finishes varies according to the year. In September, the monsoon gradually clears away, usually finishing by the end of the month. The wind changes, the skies gradually turn blue again, and the beautiful verdant Nepalese autumn begins.

This is the overall pattern of the year's weather, though within this general framework there are considerable differences caused largely by topographical variation within the country, and the country's overall relation to the path of the monsoon-bearing winds, which it is of some interest to consider.

Throughout the monsoon period, there is a general east to west decline in the amount of rainfall, and parts of the west and north of the country receive very little rainfall at all at this time of year. The east of the country receives the highest quantities of monsoon rain as a result of the pattern of flow of the winds from the southeast, which deposit much of their load at that part of the country since they reach it first. The first major barrier to the passage of the winds is the 8000 foot range of the Mahabharat Lekh. These hills force the monsoon clouds considerably higher than they have had to go since leaving the Indian Ocean, so that much of their rainload is deposited on the southern slopes of these hills. Consequently, those parts of Nepal that lie behind higher peaks of the Mahabharat Lekh receive relatively little rain, as they are in a partial rain shadow. Other areas, such as Pokhara and the southern slopes of Annapurna, receive considerably more rain during the monsoon because the

Mahabharat range is particularly low just south of here. In addition, the Pokhara area suffers from many more thunderstorms at other times of the year, because of its peculiar position. The proximity of a hot, low-lying valley to 26,000 foot peaks causes considerable air turbulence with resulting thunder and rain.

When the monsoon reaches the Himalayas, it is forced up the slopes or channelled into the valleys. The air reaching the slopes has to rise quickly, and therefore these areas are very wet. The picture in the valleys is often more complex; the air rises more slowly, so that there is less tendency to precipitate, though at the same time there is often a strong wind in the valley, or an updraught from the heat, either of which tends to clear the clouds. It is not infrequent, therefore, for a valley bottom to have a thin strip of cloudless sky above it, closely following its course into the mountains. The shoulders of the valleys, therefore, receive more than their fair share of rain as the clouds are forced onto them from the valleys. Higher up the valleys, the clouds have lost much of their rainload, and the precipitation in these areas may not be great, though there is continual cloud and drizzle here. Those high valleys which turn to run from east to west behind the main peaks – the inner valleys – may receive very little rain during the monsoon. The trans-Himalayan area protected by the great peaks of Dhaulgiri and Annapurna, known as Mustang, and further west, Dolpo, is semi-desert in appearance with vegetation and agriculture much more akin to Tibet or the Karakoram.

So within Nepal, as in most countries, there are endless variations in weather in different places and at different times; but the beauty is that, once one knows the geographical and seasonal pattern, it is more or less possible to have the weather of your choice.

In summary, the autumn is clear, sunny and warm, cooling towards winter which is clear and cold. Later in the winter, around January or February, snow begins to fall in the mountains with light rain in the lowlands, gradually dying out as spring comes. March and April are clear and sunny, though gradually dust begins to obscure the distant views. May is very hot and dusty, and thunderstorms are quite frequent in the evenings, increasing towards June. In June, usually about the middle of the month, the monsoon arrives and continues on and off until September or October. The temperature throughout the monsoon is high, rainfall is heavy, and it is the time for flowers and butterflies. Walking is made difficult by mud, landslides, broken bridges, floods and leeches, and it is not a popular time for visitors, though it has much to offer.

Travelling around the Kathmandu Valley

It has been said that there are in the valley 'more temples than houses, and more idols than men', and you need only walk in the backstreets of Kathmandu to see this. Everywhere in the valley, there are temples, idols and shrines, around springs and hilltops, palaces and public meeting places, and fields and private houses.

There are three main towns in the valley, each separate and distinct, though Patan and Kathmandu are gradually merging into each other. Their main highlights are discussed below.

Kathmandu

To appreciate Kathmandu, you need to walk or cycle, with plenty of time to change your plans. All the back streets are full of activity, with shrines, temples and wood-carved windows everywhere, but among the more important sites you will see the following: Durbar square, the heart of Kathmandu, containing numerous fine buildings, including Hanuman Dhoka palace, the old residence of kings, built in the seventeenth century, where King Birendra was crowned in February 1975; the palace of the Living Goddess, Kumari, the virgin goddess who lives here until puberty; Taleju temple, open to the public only during the festival of Durga Puja, and then only if you are a devout Hindu; Shiva Parvati temple, dedicated to Shiva and Parvati, daughter of the mountains.

Elsewhere in the city, there are numerous things to see, including The National Museum and natural history museum, which are not grand museums, but serious attempts to record Nepal's heritage; Swayambunath, set in a striking position on a hill on the edge of the city, is one of the oldest known Buddhist sites, and today it consists of a series of imposing temples and buildings around a central courtyard, reached by an enormous flight of steps. Typically, there are Hindu shrines within the complex, but it is primarily a Buddhist site, and it really comes alive on Buddhist festival days.

Bodnath Stupa, to the northeast of Kathmandu, is another ancient Buddhist site. Guru Rimpoche, of Bhutan fame (see Chapter 7) is said to have had a hand in building the stupa, in one of his many incarnations. Today, it is an enormous symmetrical white stupa, surrounded by a circles of shops and houses, inhabited largely by Tibetans. Nearby is the Kopan monastery and centre of religious learning. The whole complex has retained very close ties with Tibet and Tibetan Buddhism.

Pashupatinath temple lies on the banks of the Bagmati river, the holiest river in Nepal, and it is one of the most important Hindu shrines in the country. Cremations are regularly performed here, on the ghats by the riverside, and the ashes eventually flow into the Ganges, mother of all rivers. Access to many parts of the temple is closed to non-Hindus.

Patan

Patan is the second largest of the valley's main towns, just across the river from Kathmandu. Walking or cycling around is, again, the best way to see the city. Durbar square is in the centre of Patan with a large amount of varied and interesting buildings and courtyards, and, unlike the Durbar squares of Kathmandu and Bhadgaon, it is also a thriving market place. The buildings include the Royal Palace, built in the seventeenth century, and the Krishna Mandir temple, an outstanding example of a Shikhari style of temple.

In Mahabaudha temple each brick carries an image of Buddha, and Hirayana Varna Maharihar was built in the twelfth century in dedication to Buddha, and has a roof made of gold. Rudra Varna Mahabihar is noted for its artwork and images of Buddha. Elsewhere in Patan, there are the Jawalkhel Tibetan refugee camp where the Tibetans have their own little community, and traditional crafts are made, and the zoo, which is not the best zoo in the world, but it gives a useful idea of some of the native mammals and birds.

Bhadgaon

Bhadgaon is the third of the valley's main cities, much smaller and more medieval and unspoilt than the other two. It is situated on a small hill overlooking the valley, and we have found it to be the most interesting of the three cities. It is, at present, undergoing an extensive and sensible restoration programme in a co-operative effort by Nepal and Germany. There are three main squares here.

Durbar square, contains the palace of fifty-five windows and the Golden Gate (a lavishly decorated gate, often considered to be the best piece of artwork in Nepal). There are the temple of Batsala and the column of Bhupatindra, who built most of Bhadgaon in the late seventeenth century. There is also an art gallery and museum, containing some beautiful and rare paintings and manuscripts.

Nyatapola square contains the Nyatapola temple, the tallest pagoda temple in Nepal, and also the unusual rectangular-based Bhairavanath temple.

The Dattatreya square contains the Dattatreya temple which is one of the oldest remaining temples in Nepal, built in 1427, and the Pujahari Nath monastery, with its beautifully carved peacock windows.

Elsewhere in the valley, outside the three main towns, a number of other places are well worth a visit. The Changunarayan temple is beautifully situated in a site that has had religious significance for at least fifteen centuries, while the Dakshinkali temple is dedicated to the goddess Kali, and is a place of animal sacrifice. Kirtipur is a small old town, on a hill just above the University, notable as the town that defied Prithwi Narayan Shah in 1768, for which all males, except musicians, had their lips and noses cut off. Thimi, a moderate cycle ride from Kathmandu, is the home of pottery and mask-making in the valley, and well worth a visit. Godavari, to the southeast of the valley, is a beautiful place set at the base of the highest hill around the valley. It is notable for the beautiful botanic gardens there, laid out by the Japanese. It is an excellent place for a picnic or a relaxing contrast to the rest of the valley, and it is also a remarkable place to see some of Nepal's natural history, especially birds and butterflies, which both abound there (see Chapter 5 for more details).

Gokarna forest is a small area of virgin forest, just a few miles east of Kathmandu, where many of Nepal's forest wildlife species can be seen in natural surroundings.

Nagarkot, Kakani and Dhulikhel are all small villages set on the rim of the valley, and renowned for their early morning views of the Himalayas, including (just) Everest. Trips are organized from Kathmandu.

Outside the main valley of Kathmandu there are various other places, accessible by road, which are more than worth a visit, though many Asian tours get no further than Kathmandu. Foremost of these places is Pokhara, which has one of the most beautiful situations of any town in the world. It is situated on the banks of a large and beautiful lake, at only 2000 feet above sea level, yet it opens onto an astonishing panorama of high peaks less than twenty miles away,

1 The upper Langtang valley in Nepal, after a light spring snowstorm. The higher valleys of the Himalayas are all 'U'-shaped through glaciation, in marked contrast to the steep lower ravines, where glaciers have never reached.

2 A high altitude subsistence settlement at 11,400 feet in the Langtang valley, Nepal.

3 A yak-cattle hybrid in the high pastures of the Langtang valley, Nepal.

4 Bridegroom at a wedding ceremony in the high Langtang valley.
The participants are essentially Bhuddist, originally from Tibet.

5 Bob Gibbons (*left*) and companion crossing a standard Nepalese bridge over the Langtang river. In the dry season, as here, the bridges are considerably safer than they look, though they are always swept away during the monsoon.

6 The summit of Lhotse (27,890 feet) from the Tawoche glacier, in the Khumbu region of Nepal.

7   Khumjung and Khunde villages in the high Khumbu region of Nepal.
These are two of the main Sherpa villages.

8 A Sherpani porter, still elegant after a day's load-carrying at high altitude. These 'Lady Sherpas' frequently carry their children as well as a load, and do their knitting as they walk.

9 Kangtega and Thamserku (*right*) from Lobuje, just below Everest Base Camp. Khumbu, Nepal.

10 Girls from Mustang, in the far north of Nepal, share a joke in Manang village on the upper Kali Gandaki.

11   Porters on a ridge above the Modi Khola, with Macchapucchare ('Fishtail') peak towering behind. Nepal.

12 Bands playing at the Red Machendranath festival in Patan in May. The wheels of the 'chariot' bearing the god are on the left. Nepal.

13 Skilled ironworkers in action in Patan.

14   An ornately carved Newar window. Kathmandu valley, Nepal.

15 Lingam and Yoni (Hindu symbols) in Pashupatinath temple, Kathmandu valley.

16 Buddha's eyes, at the top of Bodnath stupa, in the Kathmandu valley, Nepal.

17 A dwarf blue and white iris (*Iris kumaonensis*) that appears from the dry brown earth soon after the snow has melted from the highest pastures, especially where cattle gather.

18 *Rhododendron barbatum* flowering in the high fir forest, Nepal.

19 A simple water-powered flour mill. Thamang village, Nepal.

20 The carrying habit starts young in Nepal: two Thamang boys carrying heavy baskets of foliage for their animals.

21 Porters on the lower Trisuli valley trail, central Nepal.

22 *Top left* A heraldic looking cuckoo uses a tree stripped for cattle fodder as a vantage point.

23 *Top right* The ubiquitous House crow, on a rooftop in Kathmandu.

24 *Left* The common mynah is the lowland Nepalese equivalent of the English starling. It is ubiquitous in towns and villages, constantly making its presence felt with calls and screeches.

25 Ghandrung village, lying at 6400 feet on the slopes of Annapurna. It is one of the largest Gurung villages in Nepal.

26 Annapurna south from near Ghandrung. Nepal.

27 The Tashichhodzong, in the Thimpu valley, is the seat of Bhutan's governmental and religious power.

28 Masked monk dancer at a festival at Wangdiphodrang Dzong, Bhutan.

29 Taktsang monastery, the 'Tiger's Nest', in Bhutan.

30 Taktsang monastery, the 'Tiger's Nest', perched on a ledge of a 3000 foot cliff. Bhutan.

31 Serried ranks of glassless windows in the enormous Punakha Dzong. Bhutan.

32 Punakha Dzong and an informal local market. Bhutan.

33 An archery contest outside the dzong. Archery is the national sport of
Bhutan, popular everywhere. The participants always wear the national
dress, as seen here.

34 *Above* The Paro Dzong, with the National Museum of Bhutan in the Ta Dzong, visible high on the hill behind the main monastery.

35 *Right* An old Bhutanese man in the market place. Although unusual hats are commonplace, we have never seen another like this one!

36 The ruined fortress monastery of Drukyel Dzong at the head of the Paro valley, with the snow peak of Chomolhari visible behind.

37 The beautiful interior of Rumtek Monastery, Sikkim.

38 One of Kalimpong's impressive Bhuddist monasteries.

39 Tibetan traders selling Indian goods in Darjeeling market.

and completely visible to their bases. The difference in height, of up to 24,000 feet, makes for stupendous mountain views particularly onto the great bulk of the Annapurnas and the extraordinary fairytale peak of Macchapucchare (Fishtail Mountain) only a few miles away. It is well worth getting up early for the dawn views.

The town of Pokhara itself is relatively ordinary, though there is plenty to do, and it is a pleasant and relaxing place to spend a few days. A trip on the lake in a dug-out canoe is a memorable experience, and there are other lakes and cave systems in the area to explore. It is also the starting point for several major treks. Gorkha is a small fortress town between Pokhara and Kathmandu, set high up on a ridge, with a few impressive buildings. It is particularly famous as the ancestral home of the Shah kings, beginning with Prithwi Narayan Shah, and it gave its name to the Gurkha soldiers of the British, and other, armies.

Lumbini, in the Terai some ten miles from Bhairawa, is the birthplace of Buddha, who was born here in 563 BC (not in northern India as is often stated). It is thus an internationally important shrine, and in 1967 U Thant, as secretary general of the UN, visited the site and suggested developing it. Peaceful gardens now surround the shrine.

Janakpur, in the eastern Terai, is the birthplace of Sita, wife of Rama and heroine of the great Hindu epic, the Ramayana. The temple of Janaki commemorates her birth, and is the site for thousands of worshipping pilgrims at certain times of year.

Finally, the Everest View Hotel should be mentioned. This luxury hotel, situated at nearly 13,000 feet, is surrounded by some of the world's highest peaks, including Everest, Amu Dablang, Thamserku and Kwangde. For those who do not wish to trek, but who want to experience the high mountains, this could be the answer.

Trekking in Nepal

In Nepal, one is spoilt for choice, and the final decision has to be made according to time available, physical ability, and the desire to see a particular area or feature. Nearly all the areas can be approached by STOL aircraft, and a few days' walking, so time is not too critical, though there are great advantages to walking in all the way. Many of the lower and midland areas are the most fascinating for their mixtures of people, religions and cultures, and the contrasting views of lush fields with high peaks and forests are very beautiful. At the same time one gradually gets fitter and more acclimatized as the walk goes on, in readiness for higher altitude walking ahead. In general, if you have time, it is most sensible to walk into a mountain area, and then fly out if your time is short.

The Solu Khumbu

This is the land of the Sherpas and Mount Everest, and it is still one of the most popular areas to trek in. You can fly into Lukla at 9200 feet or Syangboche at 12,000 feet, completing in a day what would otherwise be a ten to twelve day trek. The star of the trek is undoubtedly Everest, but there are many other mountains and monasteries in the area that combine to make it so attractive. In almost any view from above Namche, the peak of Amu Dablang is far more dominant and beautiful than Everest, despite being some 6000 feet lower. There are Buddhist monasteries at Pangboche, Dingboche, Thame and Tengboche, to name but a few. Of these, Tengboche situated on a spur at 13,000 feet, surrounded by huge peaks in every direction, must be one of the most beautiful places for religious study and contemplation in the world.

The main walk-in approach is from Lamosangu, on the Kodari highway, and for about nine days you trek up and down against the grain of the country (good training!) until you eventually reach the Dudh Kosi river. This first part of the trek is a kaleidoscope of villages, houses, terraced hillsides, shrines, prayer flags and mountain and forest views, at the same time whetting one's appetite with frequent views of the high peaks. It is also possible to approach via the Rolwaling valley, over the 19,000 foot Trashi Labsta pass, though this requires greater preparation and physical abilities. Approaches directly up from the Terai, via Okhaldunga, are also possible and equally interesting.

Eventually all trails lead to Namche Bazaar, the main village and focal point of the region. Slung in a small natural amphitheatre and crowned by the peaks of Kwangde and Kong Di Ri, at 11,000 feet this is the last major settlement in the area for those on the way up. There are a few lodges, shops with a reasonable range of food and equipment (much of it ditched by returning expeditions, and including delightfully unexpected items like Mars Bars, which suddenly become highly desirable after ten days' hard walking!). It is also the headquarters of the Sagarmatha (Everest) National Park. A thousand or so feet above are the villages of Khunde and Khumjung, staging posts for most of the major climbing expeditions in the area, and with particular associations with Edmund Hillary's aid efforts.

From here, the most frequently taken route is to Everest Base Camp, some three to four days away, to sit on the top of Kala Pattar (18,450 feet), a small hill on the side of Pumori. From here you can look out over the Khumbu glacier and ice fall at the massive black pyramid of Everest, now only 11,000 feet above you. There are many other peaks over 20,000 feet, and the views are stupendous. Trips to the lakes at Gokyo, and the lower slopes of Makalu are both worthwhile, and despite the fact that most of the region is over 14,000 feet, there is plenty to see for the patient and enquiring visitor. The walk in is probably the most strenuous time, in terms of hills to climb, though the trails are easy. Above Namche the slopes are gentler in the glacial landscape, but the problems of altitude are ever present. There is little in the way of shelter above Namche.

Langtang and Helambu

The Helambu region can be covered in a round trip of about nine days from Kathmandu, following trails up to about 11,000 feet where the views of the Himalayas are excellent. In the northern section of the route live Sherpas, distantly related to those in Khumbu. This is not a particularly difficult trek, and it makes an excellent introduction for those with little time (or money), or anxious not to tackle anything too difficult. The trek can be extended in various directions if desired, particularly towards Gosainkund lakes and Langtang, though this involves a 15,400 foot pass, and a long section with no villages and poor trails.

Langtang can be approached from Trisuli and Betrawati, north of Kathmandu, and readily accessible by road. This is a reasonably easy route, following the main river valley most of the way, right up to Langtang village, at 11,000 feet, or the cheese factory and small settlement at Kyangin, at 13,000 feet. Beyond Kyangin, the valley extends on for a considerable distance, without any habitation, right up to the Tibetan borders. Most maps of this section are totally inaccurate. It is then possible to return directly into Helambu over a high and rather tricky pass, often blocked by snow, or less directly via Syabru and the beautiful pilgrimage lakes of Gosainkund. Views from the lakes, towards Annapurna in particular, are superb, and it is a magical place at times. The whole area is a national park, and there are numerous interesting trails to explore, and high peaks to climb, as long as one keeps away from the Tibetan border.

North of Pokhara
This area offers two particularly good routes: the Kali Gandaki
Manang trek, and the Annapurna area.

As soon as you leave Pokhara, the scenery is dominated by the
peaks of Annapurna and Macchupucchare (which becomes increasingly fishtailed as one goes west), with the Dhaulgiri Himal
becoming more dominant as you move up the Gandaki valley.
Bananas grow against a skyline of white peaks, and sub-tropical
sunbirds nest within sight of glaciers. The Gandaki valley is literally
miles deep, well over 20,000 feet at one point, and the deepest valley
on Earth. Following the Gandaki valley to Jomson you pass right
through the backbone of the Himalayas, and cross the great
geographical, climatic and biological threshold into the dry parched
Tibetan plateau area. Within a few days, you pass through
spectacular changes of scenery and culture. From the holy shrine at
Muktinath you can climb over the 17,800 feet Thorung La, a pass
which is not too difficult but which demands advance planning. On
the top the views are simply spectacular, onto the back of Annapurna and away towards Tibet. The descent down through the
beautiful Marysandi valley, under the shadow of the Annapurnas, is
very rewarding.

A very spectacular, though less arduous trek is into the Annapurna sanctuary. In a week's walk from Pokhara you can walk
around the back of Macchupucchare, and be sitting on one of the
many glaciers that flow off the south face of Annapurna, at 14,000
feet. This trek, taking you through tidy Gurung villages, bamboo
thickets and dense forest, and with rich wildlife and excellent views,
is particularly rewarding for the effort put in. It is something of a
microcosm of Nepal.

Facilities in this area are generally good, as it has been an
important trading area for centuries, with a long history of
hospitality, but if you move into the higher altitude areas you have to
be correctly prepared. Flights to Jomsom are frequent.

Lake Rara
The usual approach into this area is by flight into Jumla, four to five
days' walk from the lake. This area is hardly ever visited by the
tourist, and has the challenge of having very little known about it. It
is ecologically distinct from eastern and central Nepal, with the
added bonus of having Nepal's largest and deepest lake. The
surrounding mountains are not so spectacular, but the whole area is

unusual, beautiful and quiet. Facilities north of Jumla are very minimal, and it is necessary to bring all you need with you. The lake can be approached from the Terai, but the logistic problems are considerable, and everything has to be carried.

Other Areas
There are many less well-known routes one can follow, away from the better-known treks, and these can often be just as rewarding, especially if you have time to spare for exploring.

One interesting trek can be followed up the Arun valley, in eastern Nepal towards Makalu, trekking from Dharan or flying into Tumlingtar. This is a quiet area, rarely visited, but with some spectacular mountain and gorge views on the upper Arun. In the far east, it is possible to trek around Ilam and onto Topke Ghola with excellent views of Kanchenjunga, though facilities are minimal and everything needs to be carried.

Other trips might include the Ganesh Himal, north of Kathmandu, with some interesting lakes and fine views, or in the Rolwaling Himal for fine high altitude walking.

3. Nepal's Past and Present

History

Nepal is an exceptionally historic country. Wherever one looks, there are artefacts or customs from bygone ages. Many of the buildings are old, some of them are very old, and it seems as though little has changed for hundreds of years. And this is somehow reinforced by the constant towering presence of the Himalayas, giving a feeling of unchanging solidity. But strangely enough, Nepal is a very young country, both politically and geologically.

About 70 million years ago, the area that is now Nepal was under a vast sea. At about this time, the continents of India and Asia moved closer together and eventually collided, giving rise to the first ripples which lifted the Himalayas out of the sea by about 1500 to 2000 feet. The rivers that flowed from these hills ran into the Ganges sea to the south and the Tibetan sea to the north. Between 10 and 15 million years ago, the early ancestors of man (Oreopithecus) made their home here, while less than a million years ago, primitive man had grouped together in small tribes on these hills and was making and using tools. The uncanny fact is that the Himalayas as we now know them were not there at the time! Primitive man lived in the area during the most rapid period of growth, between 800,000 and 500,000 years ago. There had been a steady rise in the height of the Tibetan plateau – for a time higher than the Himalayas – and the Himalayas themselves, but about 1 million years ago they began their phenomenal upward movement, and rose 10,000 feet in about half a million years, culminating in something approaching what we now see. They have not stopped growing yet, but the forces of erosion have shaped and worn them to the familiar outline of today. Activity in the area is still manifested in the scatter of hot springs throughout the country including at Muktinath, where flowing gases leak from the earth at the same point as a spring, causing 'burning water' at a shrine much venerated by Hindus and Buddhists alike. Tremors are not unusual, and the last major earthquake in Nepal in 1934 devastated a large area and killed 10,000 people in Nepal and Bihar.

It gives one a very strange feeling to look at the Himalayas and try to imagine man being there before them. Perhaps Tenzing and Hillary were not the first to climb Everest after all!

The history and legends of Nepal refer mostly to the Kathmandu valley up until the eighteenth century when Nepal was united under the Shah kings from Gurkha. Before this, there are patchy historical records extending back to the birth of the Human Buddha, Sakyamuni, in 563 BC at Lumbini, but before that we have to rely on legend.

It seems that the valley was once a deep, clear lake, full of snakes, and in which dwelt numerous deities. It was thus one of the most holy places in Asia, and pilgrims came from far and wide to pay homage. At that time the lake was called Nag Hrad (Place of Snakes) and it was covered with sacred lotus plants. One day one of the plants spontaneously emitted a sheet of flame, and its flowers shone with the colour of gold and precious stones (in another version, the primordial Buddha, Bipaswi Buddha, planted the lotus and manifested himself upon it). In either event, the lotus was recognized as the miraculous manifestation of Adi-Buddha, the godhead. A little later, a Manchurian Boddhisatva called Manjusri visited the lake to worship the godhead. After circling the lake, he decided that his followers would settle here and flourish in peace, so he drew his sword and cut a valley in the hills to the south, at the place now called Chobar (Sword-cut). The waters rushed out, carrying all the serpents with them, with the exception of the snake king, Kakotak, who was allowed to remain. Manjusri kindly carved a second, much smaller lake at Taudha, as a home for the snake king. The sacred lotus changed into Swayambhu hill, standing high above the fertile valley now exposed.

Manjusri returned to China, well satisfied with his efforts no doubt, and left behind his chief councillor Dharmakkar to establish the first city in the valley, Manjupattan (named after Manjusri, and now known as Patan). A stupa was built at Swayambhu at least 2000 years ago, though much of the structure of the present temple is of more recent origin. There is some evidence that the religious history of the site goes back considerably further than 2000 years.

We know that after Dharmakkar (Manjusri's chief councillor) came Dharmatta. He came from India, bringing with him the Hindu four-caste system, and he is said to have laid the site for Nepal's oldest and most venerated Hindu temple, Pashupatinath. After this, the valley was ruled by the Gothala (Cowherd) and Ahir (Shepherd) dynasties for an uncertain period, until they were deposed by the Kiranti tribes from east Nepal. Little is known of the Kiranti period of rule, except that during the reign of the fourteenth Kiranti king, Sthunko, that great promoter of Buddhism, Emperor Asoka, visited the valley from India, and raised a pillar in Lumbini in 250 BC to commemorate the birthplace of Buddha. He also continued to send emissaries and missionaries to Nepal who promoted Buddhism, and converted the people of the valley. Relics still remain from this period, notably the famous stupas in Patan.

The Kiranti were eventually replaced by the Lichavis, though it is not entirely clear how the change took place. The age of the Lichavis, from fourth to seventh century AD, is often viewed as the Golden Age of Nepal (still mainly referring to the Kathmandu valley) when the arts flourished and peace reigned. It is obvious that the arts did flourish, but perhaps its peaceful and golden nature have been enhanced by our lack of information and the mists of time! It is known, however, that the Lichavis came from the Uttar Pradesh and Bihar regions of India, and that they fostered the study of Sanskrit and the production of carvings, and the oldest known stone carvings in Kathmandu date from this period (the oldest is dated 388 Saka Sambat, i.e. AD 467). One of the great kings of this era was Amashuvarman, who ruled in the seventh century, though it was his daughter's achievements that are more memorable. The king of Tibet, Srong-Tsan-Gampo, ruled over a considerable area, and decided to cap his achievements by marrying princesses from the neighbouring countries of Nepal and China. Amashuvarman acceded to his request (or ultimatum!) and sent his daughter Bhrikuti to Lhasa, which Srong-Tsan-Gampo is credited with founding. Bhrikuti, together with the Chinese princess who arrived some two years later, succeeded in converting the Tibetan king to the Buddhist faith, and close ties developed between Nepal and Tibet. It seems Tibet exercised some form of suzerainty over Nepal, but it is certain at least that trade took place and that Newar craftsmen went to Lhasa and built palaces and temples and created various works of art, some of which may still be there. Strangely enough, Buddhism was later re-introduced from Tibet to Nepal.

After the Lichavis, there are several hundred years of obscure confusion with few relics or records of events. It is thought that the

Guptas of northern India held sway over the valley, in the so-called Thakuri period. Buddhist practices appear to have waned, and Tantric rites and ideas became prevalent.

In the eleventh century, we begin to see the rise to prominence of the Mallas, originally from the landed gentry of northern India, as a prelude to their later dominance of the valley. The story goes that in the late twelfth century, a certain Ari Deva was wrestling one day when he was told he had a son and heir. 'Call him Malla', the king ordained, for *Malla* means 'wrestler' in Sanskrit. Thus began the Malla dynasty, which lasted intermittently until the rise of the Gurkhas in the eighteenth century. Periodically, the Thakurs from Nawakot, a small town on the rim of the Kathmandu valley, took control until they were again ousted by intrigue, military action or popular revolt. There were peaceful periods under the Mallas, when the arts and architecture flourished and the Nepalese coinage was established, and the Malla dynasty was notable for an early example of dual rule shared between king and prime minister, and for the upsurge of Hinduism and the confirmation of stratified Brahminism (the caste system). In 1614, Lakshmi Narsingh built the guest-house of Madu-Satal from the wood of a single tree. It became known as Kasthmandap, Square House of Wood, and gave Kathmandu its modern name, changed from the older Kantipur. In 1639, Lakshmi's son Pratapa Malla came to power. This was a comparatively peaceful period, when trade flourished, and when many notable palaces and temples were built. Pratapa was unusual amongst Nepal's rulers in that he loved beauty and poetry, and an inscription of his was found on a stone near the Vishnu Mandir temple in Kathmandu. It is dedicated to Kalika and uses fifteen languages including French and English! Rule eventually passed to Pratapa's grandson, Bhaskara Malla, followed by a distant relative, Jagaj Jaya Malla. At the same time, Jaya's brother ruled in Patan, Ranjit Malla ruled in Bhadgaon, and Danuvanta ruled in Kirtipur under allegiance to Patan. Each kingdom was jostling and pushing for greater power in the valley, rather like the Greek city-states at the time of Philip of Macedonia, and it was this disunity that so weakened the valley, and encouraged the Gurkha king, Marbhupal Shah, to attack the valley in 1736.

The Gurkhas came from the town of Gurkha, in the mountains west of Kathmandu, but their origins are in India. They gradually extended their influence in the hills, until the ninth king, Marbhupal Shah, began to cast envious looks in the direction of the fertile and prosperous valley of Nepal (i.e. Kathmandu). In 1736, spurred on by his knowledge of the constant quarreling between the city-kingdoms of Kathmandu, Bhadgaon and Patan, Marbhupal attacked the valley. The king of Kathmandu, Jagaj Jaya Malla, routed the Gurkhas with his highly trained Newar troops, and Marbhupal returned to Gorkha in total defeat. He died in 1742, and his twelve-year-old son, Prithwi Narayan Shah, took over the throne, together with his father's intense desire for the valley. At first he was no more successful, but he was young and determined, and an able field soldier. He gradually consolidated his position outside the valley, signed allegiances with neighbouring chiefs, and eventually sent 2000 Brahmin priests into the valley to spread discord and unrest, or at least to fan the flames of that which already existed.

In the valley, events were moving at their usual hectic pace. Jaya Prakash had been exiled from Kathmandu by his wife, though he managed to return and have her killed. In Patan, the Newar Pradhans deposed Jaya's brother and had his eyes put out. Jaya retaliated by forcing the Pradhans to beg in the streets and parading their wives as witches. He upset Bhadgaon by seizing valuable offerings brought by pilgrims for the temples of Kathmandu, and to cap it all he summoned a leading statesman from Nawakot to Kathmandu, and had him killed for plotting with the Gurkhas (which he probably was). So when Prithwi attacked Nawakot, he was almost welcomed as a bringer of revenge, and he used Nawakot as a base for his attacks on the valley. First he attacked Kirtipur, but was repulsed when Jaya's army came to the rescue. Danuvanta, king of Kirtipur, had been let down by his masters in Patan, so he went to Kathmandu to offer his allegiance to Jaya. But Jaya was rapidly deteriorating into total insanity, and he had most of Kirtipur's nobles killed, while the rest were paraded in the streets dressed as women. At this stage Patan sent envoys requesting Prithwi to be their ruler, but he declined, suspecting a trap, and sent his brother instead. As he suspected, his brother was later deposed and murdered by the Pradhans in 1765.

Prithwi now changed tactics, and laid siege to the valley, and anyone who attempted to enter or leave was hung from the trees lining the passes. After two years of this, at a time of increasing disunion in the valley, he attacked Kirtipur again, but was again repulsed. A third attempt immediately afterwards was successful. He laid siege to the inner fortifications, and declared an amnesty in return for surrender. But when Kirtipur finally surrendered, he had all the noses and lips of all males over twelve, except for wind instrumentalists, cut off, whereupon Kirtipur became known for a while as Naskatipur, 'Town of Cut Noses'.

Prithwi now turned his attention to Patan, but progress was delayed when Jaya requested help from the East India Company, who sent a column under Captain Kinloch. They never arrived, however, prevented by the thick Terai jungle and its deadly malaria mosquitoes. So the following year, 1768, Prithwi simply waited for the festival of Indra Jatra and marched into Kathmandu when most of the population was either drunk or otherwise engaged. Patan fell soon afterwards, and Jaya holed up in Bhadgaon. The following year, the Gurkhas took Bhadgaon, and ruled the whole valley, sparing the life of Jaya, and eventually giving him a royal funeral on the ghats of Pashupatinath. Thus began the Shah dynasty's rule of Nepal. Prithwi ascended the throne in 1768, and died in 1775. He had, in twenty-three years, expanded his kingdom from Lamjung to Everest, and laid the foundations of modern Nepal with its capital in Kathmandu.

The Gurkha kingdom continued to expand after Prithwi's death, under the leadership of Bahadur Shah, Prithwi's grandson. His armies went as far west as the borders of Kashmir, as far east as Sikkim, and into Tibet as far as Shigatse. This incursion into Tibet in 1788 did not please the Chinese, and when the Gurkhas sacked the Grand Lama's palace at Tashi-Lhumpo, they counter-attacked. A fierce running battle followed, with the Gurkhas retreating as far as Betrawati, a mere day's march from Kathmandu. Bahadur Shah panicked at the thought of Chinese troops in the valley, and called for help from the East India Company. Captain Kinloch set out, without troops, to act as a mediator, but arrived to find the matter settled, and the Chinese gone. This was, no doubt, a salutary reminder to the Gurkhas of their limitations, and the presence of greater powers on their northern and southern borders.

In 1795, King Rana Bahadur had the regent (Bahadur Shah) imprisoned, and later killed. The king himself was probably insane from birth and was never popular, but his shocking conduct of marrying a Brahmin girl earned him the outrage of his people. The Brahmin priests cursed the union, despite the 100,000 rupees the king is said to have paid them to have the marriage sanctified, and the queen duly fell ill and died of smallpox. The king went berserk, raging through the temples and shrines leaving a trail of destruction such that the populace rose up and threw him out of the country. He took with him his legitimate queen Tripura Sundavi and some of his ministers, and went to Benares.

Shortly afterwards, the queen returned with the king's chief councillor, Bhim Sen Thapa, helped by the current regent, Damodar Pande. He was accordingly rewarded by being murdered, and Bhim Sen ensconced himself as prime minister, accountable only to the queen. The king returned later, only to be stabbed to death by his brother, leaving Bhim Sen in an unassailable position of power, which he retained for the next thirty years.

Nepal's efforts at expansion had become constrained by the Chinese to the north, the Sikhs to the west and the Bhutanese to the east and so their attention turned to the south. There had been minor disputes before between Nepal and the East India Company, but these turned in 1814 into a full-scale territorial war. An armistice was declared in 1815, but fighting broke out again, finally ceasing in 1816 when General Ochterlony's troops had threatened the Kathmandu valley. Bhim Sen (the prime minister) reluctantly gave up his ideas of expansion, and a treaty was signed at Segauli, defining the borders of Nepal more or less as they are today. The treaty was highly significant in two other respects, in providing recruitment of Nepalese soldiers (Gurkhas) into the British Army, for the British knew a good thing when they saw it – and providing for a permanent British Resident to be stationed in Kathmandu. One had arrived some years before, but his stay had lasted for less than a year, so the new arrangement marked the start of the strong ties that were to develop between Britain and Nepal.

Bhim Sen's power declined rapidly when the new king, Rajendra Bikram Shah, came of age, and in 1833 his appointment was not renewed at the annual review ceremony of Pajani. In 1837 he was imprisoned, and in 1839 he committed suicide. At the time, Nepal was in a turmoil, with murder and intrigue commonplace. The king was simply a figurehead being used by the various competing factions for their own ends. Out of this chaos and disunity, there arose another of the great names of Nepalese history, that of Jang Bahadur Rana. King Rajendra's queen, Laksmi Devi, had a lover by the name of Gagan Sing whom the queen wished to make prime minister, which involved the removal of the current prime minister, Mathbar Sing. The queen instructed Jang Bahadur to kill Mathbar, who happened to be Jang's uncle. Undaunted, in 1845 Jang shot him. King Rajendra, however, was outraged by the queen's behaviour, and he ordered the death of Gagan Sing. The queen was mad with grief at the loss of her lover and she summoned all the ministers, military leaders, noblemen and politicians to the Kot, a courtyard in the royal palace. Jang Bahadur arrived with three regiments of soldiers in support of the queen, and the subsequent events are known collectively as the Massacre of the Kot. The queen demanded the death of those responsible for the death of Gagan Sing, and in the ensuing battle and chaos, most of Nepal's leaders and noblemen were killed by Jang's troops, on 15 September 1846. Jang thus disposed of more or less all his rivals at a stroke, and soon after became prime minister. He eventually deposed the queen, after she had attempted to have him killed, and she and King Rajendra fled to Benares. Jang Bahadur installed King Surendra as head of state, in name only, of course, as he was virtually confined to his palace. This was the start of the Rana regime, a period of suppression of the masses and isolation from the outside world that was to last for the next 104 years, until 1951, when the Shah kings returned to full power in Nepal.

Jang Bahadur may have been a ruthless, ambitious and cunning man, but he was also remarkable for his bravery and intelligence, and even charm. He recognized the need to befriend the British, for the Sikhs had lost their war in the Punjab, and Jang had no desire to let the same thing happen in Nepal. In 1850 he travelled to England and France, meeting Napoleon III, the Duke of Wellington, and even Queen Victoria. He is said to have watched boxing matches, visited numerous factories, and been amazed by the size of English cattle and it was clearly a successful mission. He was away for a year, and on his return he visited nearly all the major shrines of India, for he was the first Hindu leader to have crossed the 'black' water in recent years, and it was important to show that he was not contaminated by the experience.

Shortly after his return, he put down an attempted plot to overthrow him, and ensured that the succession to the position of prime minister remained within the Rana family by passing from brother to brother, or, brother to cousin. This arrangement persisted until the eventual overthrow of the regime. Jang died in 1877, and was recognized at home and abroad as a formidable statesman and military leader. He had ensured that Nepal remained with the Nepalese, while at the same time ensuring that his own family retained power.

Although the Rana regime was notable for its oppressive policies and isolation from the outside world, many changes took place, and the regime had its share of far-sighted and compassionate leaders. Sati (in which the wife throws herself on the burning body of her dead husband) and slavery were abolished by Chandra Shamsher early in the twentieth century, and it was Chandra who built the vast Singha Durbar palace in Kathmandu. He was also responsible for introducing many of the exotic trees, such as Silk oak and Bottle-Brush that now line and beautify the streets of Kathmandu.

The start of the Second World War probably marked the beginning of the end for the Ranas. Unrest in the country culminated, in 1940, in the arrest of over 100 men as traitors. Four out of five ringleaders were executed for the crime of secretly contacting the Shah kings. Today these men are national heroes, read about by every school child, and immortalized in the Martyrs' Arch at Tundhikel in Kathmandu. Although this revolution was unsuccessful, the tide was turning. Gurkhas returning from the war spread the ideals of democracy and nationalism that they had learnt and seen while abroad. Great changes were taking place in India, as the British withdrew, and the new regimes in India posed a threat of Indian dominance to Nepal. Padma Shamsher yielded to pressure to relax the autocratic rule, and he introduced the Constitutional Act of 2004 (1948) with the help of Indian constitutional advisers. But the other factions of the family were alarmed at the thought of losing their power, and the Act was never implemented. Padma was forced to retire through 'ill health', and Mohan Shamsher took control. The regime sought recognition elsewhere, from Britain in particular, and they eventually won recognition as an independent state from India in 1950 when Mao Tse-Tung's threat to 'liberate' Tibet forced India's arm.

Within Nepal, things were happening fast. Two underground opposition movements had successfully organized a series of strikes, and in 1950 the two movements joined forces to form the Nepal Congress, a revolutionary movement intending to use force if necessary to topple the Ranas. This action was precipitated by the signing of the 1950 treaty between India and Nepal. On 6 November 1950, King Tribhuvan Shah diverted suddenly and unexpectedly from an excursion for a picnic into the grounds of the Indian Embassy, from where he was allowed to fly to Delhi on the 11th. He was greeted with the full honours due to a head of state, and became the spearhead of the external movement against the Ranas. The Ranas placed King Tribhuvan's four-year-old grandson, Jyanendra, on the throne, calling for recognition of the new ruler from friendly countries. India replied by officially recognizing Tribhuvan as ruler on 6 December, while Britain bided her time as she had just signed a new friendship treaty which included Gurkha recruitment clauses. The Nepal Congress stepped up the pace of the revolution, and on 7 February 1951 Mohan Shamsher bowed to the inevitable. On 15 February, the king and the leaders of the Nepal Congress returned to Nepal cheered by thousands, and by 18 February a ten-man cabinet had been appointed. The royal family had returned to power after 104 years.

The success of the revolution, and return to power of the royal family was, without doubt, a popular change, but it took many years before it became a viable, stable arrangement. Early in 1955, King Tribhuvan dissolved the cabinet and formed a Council of Ministers under the crown prince, but shortly afterwards, in March 1955, the king died while undergoing treatment in Europe, and his son Mahendra Bir Bikram Shah Deva ascended the throne at the age of thirty-five. It was a daunting task that faced one with so little experience of the outside world at a time when Nepal's politics and relationships were becoming increasingly international. Internal politics were still chaotic, exacerbated by India's policy of hostility to the Chinese, but the Nepalese gradually developed their own external policy of diplomatic balance, and in Mahendra's first year of office, Nepal was admitted to the United Nations. In an attempt to clarify his domestic political chaos, Mahendra proclaimed the first constitution in February 1959. This established a constitutional monarchy, parliament, cabinet, privy council and supreme court. Elections were held, and the National Congress Party gained a healthy majority. The king appointed its leader, B. P. Koirala as his prime minister, and the constitution was formally inaugurated on 30 June 1959.

Then, without warning, the king dissolved Parliament on 15 December 1960, arrested many of its leaders, and assumed direct control of the country himself. The reasons are still not entirely clear, but it is known that the king felt democracy was not right for the country, and that too much bickering was going on. He may also have felt that the monarchy was threatened, but we shall probably never know. He instituted a new partyless 'Panchayat' system (discussed later on in this chapter) of government with representatives from every district, with the king at the top of the tree, which began its first session on 18 April 1963.

From then on, Nepal's domestic and international politics have been stable. Mahendra made enormous strides in the areas of education, health, communications and social reform, and he opened Nepal's doors to the world. His policies reached out into the countryside such that every citizen took a pride in being Nepalese, and he shifted this nationalistic fervour firmly behind the monarchy. He died on 31 January 1972, and was immediately succeeded by his son Birendra Bir Bikram Shah Dev, whose official coronation took place three years later on the auspicious date of 24 February 1975. King Birendra was educated at schools in India and England, and at various universities in the United States and Japan, and he ascended the throne when he was twenty-seven. He married Aishwarya Rajya Laxmi Devi, the daughter of a Rana general in 1970, and in 1971 they had a son, Crown Prince Dipendra Bir Bikram Shah Dev.

He has proved to be a popular and positive leader of the Nepalese people, who has extended and accelerated his father's work. While greatly improving the domestic life of the Nepalese, he has also lifted Nepal from its isolated state into a respected role in Asian and Third World politics.

Present-day

Today, Nepal is a fascinating and chaotic jumble of medieval life and jet-age bustle, of modern hotels and an international airport next to temples and houses which may be over a thousand years old, with everything overshadowed by the unspoilt peaks of the world's highest mountains. There have been incredible changes since the early 1950s, yet much of what is best in Nepal has remained despite the changes, and the Nepalese themselves have quickly adapted to the different lifestyle that these changes have demanded. Since the hereditary Shah kings regained power, thus ending the long isolationist Rana regime, and the first tourists were allowed into the country, Nepal has been hustled into the jet age in the space of less than twenty-five years. Previously, there were virtually no outside visitors, none of the trappings of modern civilization, and hardly any roads or cars. Of course, there were no hotels as we know them, because there was nobody requiring them. Yet today, there are well over 200,000 visitors a year, thousands of miles of road, an air network, radio stations, and hotels in abundance from jungle lodges in the Terai, through the proliferation of hotels in Kathmandu, up to the 12,500 feet luxury Everest View Hotel, just a few miles from Everest. For most countries, things like this have happened gently, so that they are absorbed into the consciousness of the people, and

History of Nepal and the Kathmandu Valley

Modern Nepal
King Birendra
1951 King Tribhuvan assumes power
Gurkha soldiers fight in First and Second World Wars with British
1846 Jang Bahadur takes power –Rana regime begins
1816 Treaty of Segauli: modern Nepal's boundaries defined
1768 Unification of the valley under the Gurkha regime
Start of the Shah dynasty as rulers of Nepal

Medieval Nepal

1767 Prithwi Narayan Shah attacks Kirtipur

General disunity in the valley

1639 Mallas return to power

Prithwi first attacks valley

1585 Thakurs regain throne

1400 Mallas annexe throne

1559 Start of House of Gurkha

14th century Establishment of Rajput Ajodhya dynasty

1303 Fall of Chitor to Mohamedan armies

1100 Thakurs of Nawakot take control

Spread of Rajput survivors into Nepal

Rajput kings

Prehistory and Legend

250 BC Emperor Asoka visits the valley
Kiranti kings
Gothala and Ahir dynasties
Legend

their shortcomings appreciated soon after their benefits. Mistakes are made, sometimes rectified, and a whole complex of social and legal consciousness surrounds the development and our attitude to them. But what happens when the whole mass of modern technology and thought descends on an unsuspecting and unprepared pastoral race? The opportunities are there to avoid the mistakes and pitfalls, yet the same old desire for immediate rewards, and short-term gains without thought for the future can confound everything.

In general, Nepal has coped well with the invasion, though perhaps the most difficult times are still to come, as the development accelerates. To understand the impact and implications, it is first necessary to describe briefly the present political and economic situation in the country.

In December 1960, King Mahendra dismissed without warning the year-old, unanimously elected Nepali Congress Party (Nepal's first democratically elected government) and arrested the popular prime minister, B. P. Koirala. So ended Nepal's brief foray into democracy, and since that time, the power has remained essentially in the hands of the king – at first Mahendra and now Birendra – aided by a prime minister and a team of other ministers. Nepal is, in fact, the world's only Hindu monarchy.

The present constitution dates from 1962, when King Mahendra declared, amongst other things, that 'the sovereignty of Nepal is vested in His Majesty'. Political parties, and party politics in general, were made illegal, and shortly afterwards in 1963, the present 'Panchayat' system was initiated. This is a way of giving everyone in the country some sort of say in the running of the country, although the final say is kept clearly in the king's hands. The Panchayat is a tiered system, based on the general administrative boundaries of the country. At the bottom of the tree, there are about 4000 village panchayats (rather like parish councils) each consisting of eleven members, and sixteen corresponding town panchayats for the sixteen towns with a population of over 10,000. Each of these basic panchayats chooses a representative who will elect the eleven members of the next tier up, the district panchayat. There are seventy-five district panchayats, corresponding to the seventy-five districts, and each of these also has eleven members. They are concerned with governing and running the individual districts, without taking major policy decisions. Similarly, the district panchayats elect representatives onto the fourteen zonal panchayats (one for each of the fourteen zones covering the country),

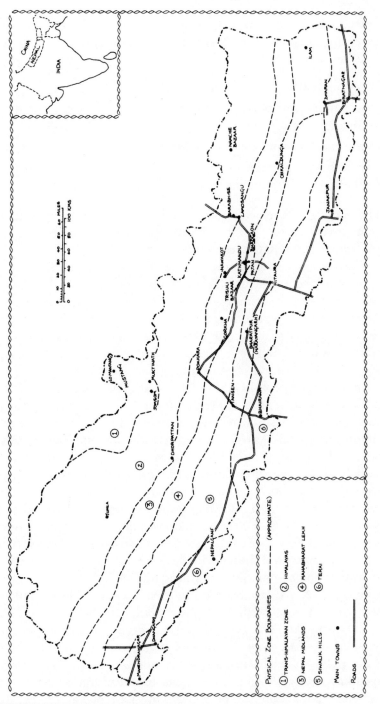

General map of Nepal showing main towns and approximate physical zone boundaries

which in turn elect representatives to the top-of-the-tree panchayat, the National Panchayat (Rastriya Panchayat) in Kathmandu. This body consists normally of:

75 representatives from the districts;

15 additional representatives from the districts with a population greater than 100,000;

16 members nominated by the king;

19 members representing various groups of Nepalese society, including youth, women and ex-servicemen.

The National Panchayat has a considerable say in proposing and debating legislation, but it is the king's decision alone as to whether any of these proposals becomes law.

The system has advantages in that it extends the law-making process in some measure right out into the farthest villages, and brings the country closer together. There is a contact for every villager right through a thread to the king. It does not work quite so perfectly, of course, and some of the villagers remain unaware of the political process, and vested interests and money play their part, as they do in all electoral systems throughout the world.

Since the present Shah kings returned to full power, one of their greatest aims has been to give the country a secure and clear-cut administrative basis to advance from, and to foster the national identity of Nepal. As we have stressed earlier, the boundaries of present day Nepal were not fixed all that long ago, and in a country with the communications difficulties of Nepal, word takes time to get around. As late as 1958, King Mahendra issued a decree asking people to refrain from referring to the Kathmandu valley alone as Nepal, as they had for so many centuries previously. When you are wedged between two of the largest nations on earth – China with 650 million people, and India with 500 million – a secure national identity becomes an important consideration.

In 1956, Nepal launched on its first Five Year Plan, and it is now well into its sixth Five Year Plan, which will take Nepal through to 1985. The general aim has been to bring Nepal up to date in as many ways as possible, in complete contrast to the Rana policy of excluding foreigners and generally attempting to keep knowledge of the outside world from as large a sector of the Nepalese population as possible. This has, of course, involved action on many fronts, particularly those of education, social reform, health, communications, agriculture, family planning, and to some extent industry.

One of the earliest problems that the government tackled was that of the land tenure system in Nepal, for it affects the amount of food that the country can produce. As a direct legacy of the Ranas, who maintained a sort of feudal system where friends and important people were rewarded with large gifts of land, the situation in the early 1950s was complex and far from satisfactory. Hardly any individual farmers owned the land they worked (in a country where 93 per cent of the population are engaged in agricultural activities), and mostly it belonged to large landowners among prominent families, who were able to extract more or less any percentage of the produce as rental, as they chose. This was sometimes as high as 80 per cent of the annual production, so the farmers were left in an exceptionally poor state, with little incentive to develop their land or use it to the full. Any surplus was simply commandeered by the landlord. The first steps towards a land reform were taken in 1955 with the preparation of the Land Reform Act 1957 which limited the rental to the landlord at 50 per cent of the produce. In addition, the tenants were accorded a certain amount of security of tenure and protection from eviction. But the Act gave no attention to the accumulation of land by the big landowners, and the hopelessness of farmers to ever own the land they tilled. So, in 1964, a further Land Act was passed which sought to limit the holding of any one person, with the idea that any surpluses would be acquired by the government for subsequent redistribution to farmers. Any single owner was limited to 25 bighas (i.e. about 40 acres), or 50 ropanis (about 6½ acres) in areas where land is very valuable, notably the Kathmandu valley. Although the value of the law has been recognized by all (except perhaps the big landowners!), it has proved to be very difficult to apply. The Nepalese farmers know little of precise measurements of area or distance, while the landlords, in some cases, went to considerable lengths to conceal the true ownership of their land. Consequently, a complete land survey was a preliminary necessity to ascertain just who really owned what. The Act is now showing real results, with a considerable area of land having been acquired and redistributed, and significantly increased productivity now that farmers can have more interest in the land they cultivate.

Through the country, a number of different basic crops are cultivated, depending largely on the local climate and altitude. In the Terai, the main crops include rice, maize, oilseed, jute, sugar cane, and other tropical crops which are grown very successfully, and can mostly be exported, from the area or out of the country. In the midland zones, the main crops are rice, millet, barley and maize, though a much wider range could be grown in the lower regions as shown by the variety grown in the Kathmandu valley, in response to the demands of hotels and restaurants. One effect of the land reform programme, with additional impetus from foreign aid, has been that the farmers of the Kathmandu valley now plant winter wheat after harvesting the rice crops where once they allowed the fields to lie more or less fallow. In the high-altitude hill regions, little can be grown in the short cool summer, and potatoes, buckwheat and barley are the main crops. There has been little increase in yield in these higher areas, though the potential is still there using different methods and new seed sources. Experiments have shown, for instance, that by using the western method of growing potatoes, instead of the traditional 'scatter it and hope' methods of the Sherpas and Bhotias, yields can be doubled immediately. There are many other ways that improvements could be made, but the people, because they live close to subsistence and cannot afford the luxury of experimentation that might be disastrous, are reluctant to accept any new methods.

This highlights another major area of development in Nepal, that of education. This is necessary not only to allow the Nepalese to fill those posts requiring education, and to bring the population to a standard of literacy and knowledge, but also to try to teach people to overcome traditional irrational fears (though many are based on sound common sense) that may have prevented worthwhile changes from taking place in the past. In 1951, there were 310 primary or middle schools in Nepal, eleven high schools, two colleges, and one technical school. Many of these were only of post-war origin. Clearly only a very small proportion of the 10 million or so people in Nepal then were receiving any education at all. In 1971, in contrast, according to the official figures, there were 7256 primary schools with an attendance of about 450,000 pupils, 1036 secondary or middle schools with an attendance of 97,000 pupils, and forty-eight colleges and the University with an attendance of 17,200 students. There has clearly been considerable progress, but the figure for primary school attendance, for instance, is only about one-third of all the children of primary school age in the country. In 1971, the rate of illiteracy was estimated to be about 76 per cent illiterate boys and men, and 96 per cent illiterate girls and women! There are still many problems to be overcome before all Nepalese children will be able to go to school. Firstly, more money is needed for the schools to be built and teachers paid. The lead in this, at least in the hill country, was taken by Sir Edmund Hillary and The Himalayan Trust, who built, equipped and financed a series of schools (and other projects) amongst the Sherpa villages. Nowadays, most schools are built by the government, but the difficulties of transport and communications are such in Nepal that it is a long process. Secondly, there is still a shortage of trained teachers. Although every year many more students graduate as trained teachers in Nepal, many of them are disinclined to return to the far rural areas to act as village teachers in the areas that need them most. And thirdly, there is the problem that in those village areas where there is both a school and a teacher, many children simply do not come to school, or come only irregularly. This happens enough in Kathmandu, but is considerably worse in the hill areas where, at certain times of the year, every hand is needed for work in the fields or the house. A teacher in such a village is lucky to get a third of his pupils on any one day.

To counteract such problems as trained teachers not returning to the villages, the government has promoted a national 'back-to-the-village' campaign, to slow migration from the hills, and to stabilize the villages as centres of life based around the panchayat system. In spite of strenuous efforts and publicity, progress is slow, and the drift to the towns still continues.

Because it lies in the semi-tropics, Nepal has an unfair share of unpleasant endemic diseases. Until quite recently, there was virtually no organized sanitation system, and the resultant combination naturally led to a high incidence of disease. Malaria was the worst of all, endemic throughout the Terai, but smallpox, cholera, typhus, diptheria, tuberculosis, hepatitis and various dysenteries were all widespread. Malaria, as we have described earlier, was so bad that it made the whole of the Terai virtually uninhabitable. Today, there are still considerable numbers of mosquitoes in these areas, but a careful programme of spraying has reduced the incidence of the disease to almost nothing. Many areas, such as the Rapti valley, have been partially cleared and resettled on what was, until recently, untouched jungle infested with malarial mosquitoes. This whole process has given the Nepalese access to their most productive areas of land, and has considerably improved the country's overall food production, though we hope that much of the remaining forest can be preserved and used wisely.

The attack on smallpox, too, has met with much success. This is by no means necessarily a killer disease in Nepal, and it is quite common to meet people bearing the scars of a previous attack. A programme of vaccination has been running for some while throughout the more accessible parts of the country, and has certainly had considerable effects on the incidence of the disease around the towns.

Many of the other diseases, though, have proved more difficult to deal with. There is no way that every person in the country can be vaccinated every six months against cholera, or every six to eight weeks against hepatitis. For these, and for other diseases with no vaccines available, the long-term solution has to be a great increase in sanitation and education into what causes these diseases. At present, there is virtually no proper sewage disposal in the country, except to an extent in Kathmandu. A long range aim of the governent is to provide pre-treated drinking water for the whole population, but at present there is hardly any, and, although villagers are invariably discriminating to some extent about which water source they use, there is often a fair chance that it is regularly or occasionally contaminated, except at the highest altitudes. These two factors mean that virtually everyone in Nepal is exposed to the risk of the water-borne diseases such as cholera and amoebic and bacillary dysenteries, and almost one child in three still dies within its first year from intestinal illnesses.

There is a degree of resistance to some of these diseases, though. Hepatitis, which may be very serious to us, is often caught and shrugged off by the Nepalese in childhood, and they suffer slightly less from the prevalent bacterial disorders, though their resistance is by no means as great as sometimes thought. So, progress is being made in the prevention of disease, but it is slow, and, to some extent, the easy part is behind and the hardest task still lies ahead. The life expectancy of the average Nepali has been raised from around twenty-five in the late 1950s to somewhere around the middle thirties now, and much of this has been achieved by reducing child deaths.

In the matter of curing diseases, progress is again being rapidly made. There are now first-class hospitals in Kathmandu and Pokhara, and a good many smaller 'hospitals' scattered around the country. Most of these, out of the towns, work under extremely difficult conditions with no electricity, difficult communications, and few facilities. But many of the social barriers against treatment are being broken down, and people are more and more ready to use these clinics, particularly when they are suffering from obvious disease or wound symptoms. It is common, as you walk through the country, to be approached by people for medical aid (though less so than in many other countries), and it is clear that shortages of doctors, nurses and hospitals is now the main problem. The number of people per hospital bed is still frighteningly high. For the visitor, though, there is likely to be no problem. Vaccinations before you go, prophylactics against malaria while you are there, the use of sterilizing tablets, and care with washing, coupled with medical insurance should cover most eventualities.

In his address to the 28th session of Rastriya Panchayat (the national parliament, in effect) in 1977, King Birendra stated that: 'My government has prepared a long-term health plan to improve the general health of the people in the country. The plan will be effectively implemented gradually. While emphasizing the need of preventative health services, my government stresses on the urgency of the development of family planning and maternity and child welfare programmes'. The government has been involved in attempts to promote family planning for some years. The present rate of population increase is about 2 per cent per annum, in other words about a quarter of a million additional people per year, and this, of course, is one of the root causes of the food shortages and environmental degradation that we can see now. The people do not take readily to family planning, because of their dependence on children for their needs in later life. They seem, though, to be more interested in it than the Indians, and progress is being made slowly.

When it comes to communications, Nepal faces more problems than almost any other country in the world. The effects of the new roads from India to Kathmandu and Pokhara have been considerable, in a country where there were no real roads at all until quite recently. The roads that there are must, of necessity, be feats of engineering because of the complex and tortuous topography. The first real effective road to be built was the Tribhuvan Rajpath, constructed in 1953 by the Indians, linking Kathmandu with India. The road itself, where it crosses the mountains south of Kathmandu, is one long series of incredible hairpin bends, much beloved by lorry drivers and overland coach tour operators! Its existence meant that freight, and tourists on overland trips, could now get to Kathmandu, and for a long time this remained the only viable overland route. There is now a quicker road which runs from Bhairawa on the Indian border to Pokhara and on to Kathmandu. Other important roads include the 'Chinese road' from Kathmandu to Kodari, and on to Lhasa (making a complete motorable road from India to Peking!), the road from Kathmandu to Trisuli, and the now-motorable Nepalese section of the Asian highway, running east–west across the Terai. At present, the road system is strongly focussed on Kathmandu, but the new east–west link will be the backbone of the road system, into which new roads will eventually link in from the north. At present, there are no roads in the eastern or western mountain areas, and it is likely that much of the Himalayas will always remain roadless. The air network is still the main way of getting into the Himalayas and hill areas.

At present, Tribhuvan airport is the only international airport in Nepal, carrying traffic, including jets, from Delhi, Bangkok and Dacca. There are limitations on the carrying capacity of the larger jets because of the difficult topography around the valley, and there is a possibility that an alternative standby airport may be constructed at Simra in the Terai, which could certainly considerably increase the volume of traffic into Nepal. It is clear that air transport is going to continue to play a very major part in the development and opening up of Nepal.

There is little doubt that the development of Nepal's industry has been hampered greatly by the poor communications. Nepal is not a suitable site to become the Industrial Estate of Asia, and it has not become so. At present, about 1 per cent of the work force is engaged in industrial work, and about 75 per cent of Nepal's industry is in the eastern Terai area, where communications with the neighbouring markets are obviously better. For this reason, and for currency reasons, Nepal is concentrating on import-substituting industries, and those using locally produced raw materials. At present, rice-husking accounts for almost half of Nepal's light industry, with jute and oil-processing next. Other processed agricultural products are made, particularly tobacco and cigarettes, yarn and textiles. The country is also concentrating on factories producing basic necessities for development, such as concrete, at the new factory near Kathmandu. Mineral wealth is constantly being explored, though as yet little of serious economic value has been turned up.

Hydro-electric power is an attractive possibility in a country with all that water constantly tumbling from the hills. There have been considerable technical problems associated with developing hydro-electric stations, particularly because of the great difference between the low winter levels and high monsoon levels. The potential is there, though, and the Trisuli power station now supplies much of Kathmandu's electricity. There are hopes that power from barrages in the Terai will be produced in quantities sufficient to export to India eventually. In 1977, King Birendra stated that: 'For the speedy economic development of the country, my government will lay special emphasis on the planning and implementation of projects to exploit the water resources that would lead to the attainment of multi-purpose objectives of hydel power generation, irrigation, drinking water, flood control, and development of fisheries'. There are plans too to develop mini hydro-electric power projects to provide power for more remote rural communities.

In the matters of industrialization and development of hydel power, as well as road-building and many of the other schemes going on in Nepal today, the country has been considerably helped by money and expertise from other countries and organizations. Since opening its doors, Nepal has done exceptionally well from foreign aid sources. In the fifteen years after 1952, the United States of America gave 100 million dollars, India gave 71 million, the Soviet Union over 20 million, and China over 18 million dollars, while many other countries including Britain gave large amounts, in addition to technical expertise. Now the largest givers of aid are reckoned to be India and China, in that order. The countries involved give an idea of Nepal's policy in this respect, and an idea of why the Nepalese have attracted so much aid. Their foreign policy is strictly neutral, so that no country has political reasons for *not* aiding Nepal, while her position is sufficiently strategic to invite support from many interested countries. Certainly, it is the general aim of the country to attract as much aid as possible, to keep all the programmes we have discussed going, and to extend Nepal's development. To quote King Birendra again: 'My government will continue to make efforts to acquire foreign aid, using the good offices of the recently organized Aid Nepal Consortium as well, for all the development activities being implemented in accordance with our basic policies and strategy of national development'. The landmarks in foreign aid in the past have involved many countries. The British have built roads and bridges, and helped to set up the radio network; the Swiss, through SATA, have contributed considerably to the way of life of the country, and they were the first to set up a cheese factory; the New

Zealanders have been much involved in hill farms, banking, other cheese factories, and in the setting-up of the Everest National Park. The West Germans are involved in a remarkable programme to restore and modernize Bhadgaon City, while the Australians have helped to improve the water supply and run Tribhuvan airport, and the French have been involved in the airline and tourist industry. The Japanese have assisted with hydro-electric projects, while the Americans, Indians and Chinese have been involved in many different projects, both constructional and social. International organizations, too, have played their part, such as the various United Nations agencies, who are closely involved in many projects in Nepal today.

Politically, it is expedient for Nepal to maintain friendly relations with as many countries as possible, and in particular to remain equally friendly with its two huge neighbours, China and India. Over the last thirty years, Tibet, Bhutan and Sikkim have all been 'infiltrated' to a greater or lesser degree, while there have been continuing troubles in the mountain areas between India and Pakistan. Nepal clearly wishes to maintain her political independence and freedom, yet it is not in a position to do this by strength alone. Traditionally, she shares much more in common with India than with China, and relationships there are generally good, though the history of Indo-Nepal relations is fraught with disagreements. The recent changes in leadership in India will, no doubt, have considerable effects on the relationship, though the way things will develop is not yet clear. As recently as May 1977, the Nepalese prime minister, Dr Tulsi Giri, complained that the Indian press and some Indian leaders had shown far too much interest in matters 'wholly within Nepal's jurisdiction' and he lashed out at the Indian press for 'taking recourse to outright lies'. In other ways, Nepal has preserved her differences from India, with a ten-minute time difference, quite a significant difference in the value of the rupee in each country (though Nepal is very much affected by currency fluctuations in India), quite a different foreign policy (for instance, Nepal maintains relations with Israel, while India does not), and, of course, a different language. Many people in the west think of Nepal as part of India, similar to, say, Kashmir, but this is very far from being the case, and the thought would not be welcome to a Nepali.

Nepal's relations with China, on the other hand, have been generally much less close until recently. Before 1950, China was, of course, a good deal further away, and had little effect on Nepal. The situation is very different now, and Nepal naturally maintains close diplomatic links with China. There is a road link from Kathmandu (not to mention the rest of the Indian continent) right through to Lhasa, and on to the rest of China, and border clashes between India and China over the last twenty years have emphasized both Nepal's fragility and her strategic importance. China's superiority in these clashes in fact led to a considerable improvement in the relations between India and Nepal, as India rapidly realized how important Nepal was, and quickly moved to 'sweeten up' the Nepalese! Many Nepalese, especially in the hills, distrust the Chinese, both for historical reasons, and because they have heard of the Chinese destruction of the Tibetan Lamaist monasteries and way of life. But the Chinese are excellent at producing good publicity material and handing it out free, and many houses in the mountains now have pictures of smiling Chinese and Tibetans working together in the sunlit fields, or in front of the Pergola, and younger generations of Nepalese may well come to think differently. The Chinese take-over of Tibet certainly had considerable repercussions in Nepal's trade patterns, though many of them were inevitable anyway in a changing world. Previously, there was a flourishing trade in salt, yaks, potatoes etc., between various hill districts and Tibet, but now only a few licensed traders can cross the border, and what they have to offer is much less in demand. Most Nepalese traders now seem to bring back the 'very good Chini shoes'. Probably the Sherpas were hardest hit by the changes, but they have found an alternative profitable niche elsewhere, of course.

On 2 June 1976, aviation history was made when a RNAC Boeing 727 flew from Kathmandu over the Himalayas to Tibet, and on beyond Lhasa to Chengtu in Szechuan, China. King Birendra was also the first ruling monarch to have been invited to visit Tibet, and this perhaps indicates the importance of close ties to both countries. It was a historic visit. The fact that King Birendra made a state visit to the Soviet Union in the same year, and also established diplomatic relations with Middle Eastern countries, shows just how successful Nepal's policy of non-alignment is. Perhaps Nepal's only difficulty with China, in recent years, concerned the Khambas. The Khambas are a mixture of tribes, particularly from the province of Kham in eastern Tibet, who were fighting an extensive and effective guerilla war in Tibet against the occupying Chinese troops. Eventually, they came to make their base in Mustang, that almost Tibetan region at the north of central Nepal, whence they could retire safely to lick their wounds when necessary. Their attacks, with the rumoured support of both the CIA and nationalist China, eventually became so successful that China, it is believed, leaned heavily on Nepal to do something about it. Nepal's own army eventually took action, and the area to the north of Jomsom was closed to foreigners until 1976. Now many Khambas have been resettled, and live very different lives in lowland Nepal, and it seems probable that all guerilla action has ceased.

Perhaps Nepal's best international advertisement is its open tourist industry, which has developed so rapidly and inevitably. Over 200,000 people, of all nationalities, are now likely to visit Nepal in any one year, and this is now the country's biggest earner of hard foreign currency. It is clear to anyone that, unless there is some unexpected dramatic change, tourism is going to play a very big role in Nepal's development, as it already has. Gradually the whole country will be opened up, and the effects on the economy and way of life of the people will be (perhaps already are) immeasurable and far-reaching. The government's commitment to tourism is inevitable, and much appreciated by all those who have now had the chance to visit this extraordinary country.

4. The People of Nepal, their Religions and Festivals

The great complexity of the racial, ethnical, cultural, religious and linguistic variety found among the people of Nepal makes an appreciation within a chapter impossible. Some groups have been studied extensively, while others, particularly those in the west, are still virtually unknown. As Professor Tucci pointed out, 'the ethnographical study of Nepal despite the many researches undertaken is still one of the most complex in the world'. We can only suggest the main outlines, discuss a few of the major groups in detail, and hope that it stimulates your interest to find out more.

The most obvious groupings are the two racial groups of the Tibeto-Nepalese and the Indo-Nepalese roughly corresponding to Mongolian and Caucasian; those that originated from the north, China and Tibet, and those from the south, predominantly Indians. This division also coincides almost directly with a linguistic division: Tibeto-Burman speaking and Indo-Aryan speaking. These two groups can be further divided and classified into smaller groups distinguishable by characteristics such as clothes and decorations, lifestyle and type of houses, customs and religion. Though the national language is Nepali, nearly all these groups will speak their own particular tongue.

For clarity, we can divide the country into three altitudinal and agricultural zones, each supporting fairly distinct racial groups: the Terai, the middle hills and valleys, and the inner Himalayan valleys. In the middle hills and valleys, where there is a cool to warm temperate climate, 60 per cent of the population live today. It is here that the original Nepalese tribes settled and found sanctuary, protected to the north by the Himalayan chain and to the south by malarial jungle. Since the time of the earliest settlers, there has been a continuing influx of people seeking refuge or a new way of life, often driven from their homes by invading armies. Generally these influxes have been peaceful, for the barriers have deterred invading armies, and the settlers have been absorbed into the life of the hills. There have been occasional far-reaching internal changes, such as when Prithwi Narayan Shah invaded the Kathmandu valley in the eighteenth century, but such events were few and far between. Many of the settlers have been high caste Hindu Brahmins or Chetris, and they brought the Hindu caste system with them. The Brahmins have remained almost pure, while the Chetris have mixed, forming new caste variations.

In the higher valleys, there has been less pressure, until the recent influx of refugees from Chinese Tibet, though there has always been a trickle of settlers from Tibet, some of whom have become distinctive Nepalese groups such as the Sherpas. Today, the hills are slowly depopulating. The eradication of malaria in the Terai, together with industrialization both there and in the Kathmandu valley, is attracting large numbers of hill people to these areas with far-reaching social and environmental consequences, such that the government has had to initiate a 'back-to-the-village' campaign, partly to counteract this movement (discussed in the previous chapter).

A number of factors have affected, and continue to affect, the distribution of the Nepalese people, but generally we can say that the Indo-Nepalese people cover most of the midlands and the whole of the Terai, while the original Nepalese groups are found in the higher altitudes of the midlands, and the Tibeto-Nepalese are mainly in the high Himalayas in the favourable valleys and along the trade routes.

Although we shall describe some of the major groups as though they were separate cultural entities, in fact few groups live in complete isolation from others, with interaction and interdependence varying according to geographical proximity, cultural similarity and trade requirements. In nearly all cases individual groups have been influenced by one or more other groups, and there is a great deal of social, economic and cultural interchange.

The influence of the two highest Hindu castes, the Brahmins and the Kshattriyas (or Chetris as they are called amongst the hill races) have been considerable. Apart from being considerable land owners and businessmen, they are prominent in many religious and social aspects. Consequently many others groups have attempted to emulate them in an effort to raise their own status. At the same time education, vastly improved communications and transportation systems, the law and the panchayats, are breaking down the caste system and the tribal system. Cross-caste marriages are far more frequent now and the present panchayat system (see Chapter 3) pays no attention to caste or creed in its recruitment and elections.

Instead of Nepal being, as it once was, a land of isolated tribes and rigid caste, it is now developing a proud national identity with a far more flexible attitude towards the mixing of class, caste and creed. There are undeniable distinctions between certain groups, and these are desirable in the broad traditional and cultural sense, but at least Nepal is no longer thought of as just the Kathmandu valley.

The People of the Terai

As explained in Chapter 2, the lowland zone of Nepal, bordering India along the whole of the southern Nepalese border, is a strip of the Upper Ganges plain known as the Terai. Conditions here are very different to those in the mountains and hills of Nepal; communications and access are reasonably good, particularly into India; the climate is sub-tropical with frosts unknown, and the alluvial soil is good and easy to cultivate. Not so very long ago much of the area was uninhabitable on account of the dreaded malaria, but a concerted programme has more or less wiped this out, and the consequent social and ecological changes have been dramatic.

Interchange with India is considerable. Many of the people are recent settlers of Indian origin, and their social organization and language tends to reflect those of the neighbouring part of India, from Bengal to Uttar Pradesh. The predominant religion is Hindu, more strictly adhered to here than in the hills, with Brahmins and Rajput Kshattriyas prominent, though there are a few Moslems too.

Of more interest for our purpose here are the indigenous or long-established people of the Terai, notably the Tharus.

The Tharus
With nearly half a million people, the Tharus are the largest of the indigenous groups living in the Terai. Their main area of settlement is traditionally the strip of forested country at the interface between the Terai plain and Siwalik hills, though they extend southwards onto the plain, and inhabit similar country beyond the Nepalese borders. They have their own language, influenced by neighbouring Indian languages such as Hindu, and their religion is basically animistic, with elements of Hinduism incorporated into it. They believe strongly in the Evil Eye, ghosts and spirits, and each family

worships a family deity, or *Mainyan*, usually represented by a strange mixture of earth, cotton threads and cane sugar, often with a gold coin or piece in the centre of the resulting lump.

They are mainly Mongolian, though this is far from clear-cut, and they have a number of non-Mongolian physical features. Their origin is not entirely certain; it seems probable that they are the descendants of Rajput settlers fleeing from the Muslim invasions of India in the twelfth century as the Tharus themselves claim – but it may be that their history in the Terai stretches back much further than that. At all events, they have developed a significant resistance to malaria and were able to settle in heavily infested districts without major ill-effects.

The Tharus are essentially farmers, nowadays usually as tenants to wealthy landowners or moneylenders, though many are turning to more lucrative work. Their methods of farming are generally primitive, and shifting cultivation is still practised in some areas.

Their whole lifestyle is still very much undisturbed by the march of progress, but one wonders how long it will remain so as roads, industry and tourists penetrate and pervade the Terai. The Tharu marriage ceremony is complex. Marriages are monogamous, usually arranged by the parents when the partners are still young, though the girl is often older than the boy, who may be as young as six or seven. In Chitwan, it is not uncommon for a young man to have to work for a few years for the parents of his intended bride. An intriguing feature of the marriage occurs when the bride comes to leave for her husband's house; her parents present her with a torch and a cup of poison – the torch to find her way with, and the poison in case she should ever fall into the wrong hands!

Eastern Tharus generally cremate their dead on a convenient riverside, but western and central Tharus generally bury them, sometimes in traditional communal burial grounds. An unexplained feature of the burial ceremony is that the men are buried face down in the earth, while the women are buried face up, both on a white cotton sheet.

Their houses are often very large, but simple in construction; one storey huts with mud (or dung) – plastered bamboo walls, and thatched roofs. These are kept remarkably clean and food and utensils are hung from the roof to keep them clean and safe.

Other Terai Peoples
Although the Tharus are far and away the largest indigenous Terai

group, there are a number of other small, but generally distinct groups of people. Some of these share common characteristics, and possibly common origin, with the Tharus. The Daruwars, Majhis and Darais share the same partial immunity to malaria, but they are essentially fishing and river people, clustered in a few small settlements around the main rivers, often penetrating far upstream into the Mahabharat or Siwalik hills. Their lifestyle is primitive and simple, and they are exploited mercilessly by unscrupulous neighbouring traders and moneylenders. Probably as a result they are shy and retiring, fearing strangers.

The Rajbansi are primarily farmers. They are the remnants of the once-powerful Koch nation, overcome by the British in India and the Shahs in Nepal. They have become split by some adopting Hinduism (the true Rajbansi), some adopting Islam and becoming Musalman, and others retaining their original Koch religion and customs. Although there are few Rajbansi people in Nepal, they are still present in sizeable populations in India.

The Satars are a small group of semi-nomadic peoples, living as hunters and primitive farmers, frequently straying between Nepal and Bihar. They live simple lives in small well-organized forest villages, set apart from the other Terai races.

The People of the Middle Hills and Valleys

The Newars

These are the traditional indigenous people of the Kathmandu valley. They are a large and influential group, estimated to have over 400,000 members, many of whom live in the Kathmandu valley. They are far from clear-cut ethnically, though they are considered to be a cultural entity, with all the groups sharing certain similarities despite differing religions and origins.

Their origins remain uncertain, despite much research. They include both Mongolian and Mediterranean types, and it is possible that they may have been in the Kathmandu valley in prehistoric times, later absorbing varied influxes and influences into their culture. They speak both Newari (a Tibeto-Burman language) and Nepali (Indo-Aryan) as their mother tongue.

Their religious and caste affinities are complex. They may be either Buddhist or Hindu, with both religions occurring even within a small area. Probably they were Buddhist initially but the influence of powerful Hindus in the Kathmandu valley meant that Hindus enjoyed greater prestige and there was a gradual shift to Hinduism over the centuries, though there was never any serious antagonism or persecution. Their religious observances, festivals and even buildings have become mixed and intertwined, with each absorbing elements of the other, leading to the occurrence of many paradoxes throughout the valley, so puzzling to the visitor who is familiar with one or other religion. Many temples contain gods of both religions side by side. At home, however, the personal and domestic worships remains distinct between the religions.

The caste system is quite strictly adhered to, with Buddhist and Hindu groups each having their own more or less equivalent rankings, though Hindu equivalents tend to have slightly more status. One of the more interesting large groups is the Jyapu caste of traditional farmers. They are responsible for the production of the high yields of crops from the valley floor, and are recognizable away from their fields when they carry two baskets full of produce or a yoke over their shoulders. They never use bullocks, in contrast to many other farming people of Nepal, and their main farming implement is, apparently, the hoe.

The Newar marriage ceremony contains one particularly interesting feature. The first ceremony that a girl undertakes is marriage to the 'Bel' fruit, and this is for life. Subsequent marriage to a man is thus considered to be less binding, and divorces are arranged simply by the wife giving back to the husband the gift of Areca nuts that she received when she married him. The origin of the custom is not clear, but it would appear to be one of those devious customs that have developed amongst Buddhists and Hindus to enable them to avoid their religious strait-jackets while still complying with the letter of their religions! The employment by Buddhists of people to kill their animals for them is another, encouraged by expediency rather than hypocrisy.

Many of the great ceremonies of the Kathmandu valley seen by the visitor are predominantly Newar ceremonies and these include Indra Jatra, Gai Jatra and Rath Jatra (in Patan), though naturally the Newars celebrate more general ceremonies, such as Tihar and Dasain (discussed later on in this chapter).

Newar houses, at least in outlying villages, are large with several storeys, built close together along cobbled streets. They tend to have numerous large doorways and windows, with elaborately carved woodwork for the wealthy. They are normally tiled or with slates, except for the very poor, whose houses are thatched. In Kathmandu, the houses tend to be built in quadrangles, often with a shrine in the centre.

The dress of the Newars is varied. Jyapu men wear the traditional Newar suit, without a western-style jacket. Many older men wear the Nepali trousers, but with a suit jacket over it, and this is official government dress. Younger men often wear western clothes of varying styles. The women wear saris and blouses generally, though Jyapu women wear their home-made saris in a slightly different style.

The Kirantis

The Kiranti people, though often mentioned in the historical chronicles of Nepal, are but little-known outside their country. They are in fact the second largest ethnic group in Nepal (the Tamangs are the largest), living mainly in east Nepal. They are a loosely defined group, consisting mainly of the Rai and Limbu peoples. They have their own language, Kiranti, which is of the Tibeto-Burman type, their features are Mongolian, and they are probably Tibetan in origin, though they have been in Nepal for a very long time. It is known, for instance, that they ruled the Kathmandu valley until about the second century AD, since when they were more or less 'lost' until the Shah kings encountered them in the late eighteenth and early nineteenth centuries. The trek to Everest from Lamosangu passes right through Kiranti territory.

The Tamangs

With something over half a million people, the Tamangs constitute the largest ethnic group in Nepal, according to the last census. They inhabit the middle and higher hills over most of the country, especially in the east and centre, though a few live in the Terai or the highest valleys. Their language is Tibeto-Burman, but like most of the long-established Nepalese groups, their origin is obscure. Most probably they came from Tibet, as it is said they were formally known as Bhotes (people from Tibet) until the general name of Tamangs was given them since many of them were horse-traders (Tibetan: *Ta*-horse, *Mang*-trader).

They usually make their living as self-sufficient farmers, growing maize, millet, potatoes, wheat, barley and rice at lower altitudes, and keeping domestic animals. Their great strength and stamina as load-carriers have led to a demand for their services as porters both for wealthy Nepalis and visiting expeditions and tourists.

Their religion is essentially Buddhist, in keeping with their Tibetan origin. Their Lamas are trained in Lamaist techniques, and there are Ghyangs (Buddhist temples) in every Tamang village. They inscribe stone tablets with prayers and build them into wayside walls and shrines, known as *Hikis*. These are a familiar feature of trails through Tamang areas, and they are often sited on a prominent pass or hilltop. The Tamangs observe some Hindu feasts such as Dasain, though this does not indicate a particular trend away from Buddhism.

Their marriage customs are broadly similar to those of many other Nepali peoples, and may be by arrangement, capture or mutual agreement. Arranged marriages are usually reserved for the very rich. In capture marriage, a boy may capture a girl if she has refused his initial advances, but if she still refuses after three days, she is free to go back to her parents. Marriage by mutual agreement is much the most common method, although the parents usually do the asking and arrange the details. Polyandry is forbidden, though polygamy is practised occasionally. Their lifestyle is generally fairly promiscuous and most things are tolerated, as long as two members of the same clan are not involved.

Tamang villages have a characteristically tidy appearance. The houses are squarely built with stone walls and usually wooden shingle roofs, occasionally slate. They are most often two-storeyed, with a balcony on the upper floor. The streets and steps are neatly stone-paved and lined with shaded resting places (Chauthara) for the weary load-carriers.

The Tamangs are becoming more educated, and a minority are veering away from the traditional agricultural way of life to take up jobs in such industries as tourism, as guides, sirdars or porters. One Tamang even obtained a PhD degree recently, though any form of higher education is rare.

The Magars

The Magars are another large group of central and western Nepal hill people, numbering rather over a quarter of a million strong. They live mainly in the hill areas north of Pokhara and around Gurkha, normally at lower altitudes than their neighbours, the Gurungs, extending in places down to the Terai, though a more Tibetan sub-group, the Nupri, lives on the high slopes east towards Ganesh Himal.

Like most Nepalese hill tribes, they live mainly as self-sufficient agriculturalists, growing the normal middle altitude crops such as millet, buckwheat, maize and wheat, with rice lower down, and keeping domestic flocks. They are also skilled craftsmen and habitual traders. The most notable change in their lifestyle has been their considerable recruitment into foreign armies as Gurkha soldiers. Their qualities of hardiness and drive were soon recognized, but they also possess great qualities as leaders. Most villages now have a number of active 'Gurkhas', and many on pensions, such that this is an essential financial buttress to the community, subsidizing the more precarious subsistence agriculture.

They are mainly Hindu in their beliefs, closely following the Brahmin-Chetri style of Hinduism, though Magars at higher altitudes are often Buddhist. Their houses are generally two-storeyed, usually thatched, and generally oval or sometimes round, washed with ochre or red mud, though in the east of their range the houses are usually white and never round.

The Gurungs
The Gurungs are ethnically related to the Magars, and in many ways their lifestyles are similiar. They too live in the hills of west central Nepal, mainly on the slopes of the Annapurnas, with their villages perched high on sunny slopes. Many took advantage of the eradication of malaria from the Terai, and they were amongst the first to colonize the fertile plains. They are also primarily agriculturalists, but they too have been widely recruited as Gurkhas, and this is now the tribe's most important source of income. They are great sheep farmers, with each village having a number of commonly owned roving flocks, and a number of customs and restrictions have developed around the use of different types of land by sheep from other villages.

Their origin is uncertain, though it is clear that they have been long-established in Nepal. They are generally Mongolian in features, though clearly differentiated from Tibetans. Some speak a Tibeto-Burman dialect, while others have lost it. They are a clear-cut ethnic group, though, with their traditional dress (a short blouse tied across the front with a short skirt wrapped round the waist for the men, and a tied cotton blouse and dark red sari for the women) and customs, and there are believed to be about 150,000 of them, almost entirely within Nepal.

Their marriage arrangements are unique in Nepal. Cross-cousin marriage is preferred, and in some cases compensation is payable if this is not observed. Son to father's sister's daughter is preferred. Normally there is a free choice into cross-cousin marriage, though parallel cousin marriage is prohibited. The usual negotiations precede marriage, but the couple don't immediately go and live together. The wife goes to the husband's home for a few days, and then returns home, where the husband visits her and so on until the wife has a child, when she, it, and a dowry go to live permanently with the husband at his family home. Long before this, the early mutual attraction that may eventually lead to marriage frequently has its beginnings in an unusual Gurung institution known as *Rodi*. This is a sort of club for boys and girls from ten or eleven up to about eighteen, supervised by an adult. The members work together in the fields, and often spend the evenings together. Boys' Rodis may make visits to girls' Rodis in a nearby village, especially if someone already knows one or two of the girls there. Everything is very free and easy, and needless to say many marriages find their beginnings here.

The Thakalis

Although very small in numbers (probably about 5000 Thakali-speaking members), the Thakalis are an interesting group of people, frequently encountered by people visiting Pokhara or trekking up the Kali Gandaki. Their home area, the Thak Khola, is the high valley of the Kali Gandaki, though now they are much more widely spread. Their welcoming hospitable inns – Bhattis – are a feature of the Pokhara area appreciated by many, and a few have spread down as far as the Terai. Many left their home area in the last century when heavy taxes on their salt trade monopoly made life very difficult, and since then changes in Tibet and within Nepal itself have caused many to move elsewhere. They are great traders and entrepreneurs, and seem happy to move wherever the opportunities are.

Tukche is traditionally the main village (the word *Tukche* derives from the Tibetan for salt-trading grounds), but most better-off Thakalis have moved away to be replaced by Tibetan refugees and others. The Upper Gandaki is generally dry, as a largely trans-Himalayan area (see Chapter 2), so the way of life is quite different to that of the hill people on the south slopes, and more akin to Tibet or the western Himalayas. At highest altitudes, apricots are an important crop, but agriculture is difficult, and trading takes its place. Lower down, more traditional crops such as wheat and buckwheat are grown. The houses are whitewashed and flat-roofed, in contrast to those in monsoon areas, and built close together.

Thakali origins are not entirely clear. They are Mongolian people with a Tibeto-Burman language (Thakali), and are related to Thakuris. Their religion is a blend of Jhankrism, Buddhism, Hinduism and occasionally Bonism, with Jhankrism as the dominant religion. Thakalis celebrate their own festivals, rather than those celebrated throughout Nepal generally. Considerable upheavals and changes are taking place in Thakali culture at present. There is a strong trend away from Buddhism, and things Tibetan, and other influences are having an effect. It remains to be seen whether they will persist as a true cultural and ethnic unit.

There are many other people who may be met in the middle hills, including many small tribes and others hitherto unstudied. Brahmins and Chetris are scattered throughout the lower and middle hills, in odd houses in other peoples' villages, or in their own villages. They generally keep themselves apart from the local people, and are not always popular.

The higher altitude people amongst the middle hill peoples such as the Thakalis and Gurungs, grade, both geographically and culturally, into the groups we have arbitrarily separated as Himalayan people, and there is not necessarily a clear distinction.

The People of the Himalayas

We are talking generally here of people who habitually live above 9000 feet (and up to 16,000 feet) in the higher valleys. They are strongly Tibetan influenced, and frequently of Tibetan origin, though the general term Bhote or Bhotia people (i.e. Tibetan) is misleading and inappropriate, and it has come to be used as a rather sneering derogatory term. Amongst the Himalayan people there is a wide variation of cultures and languages, and there are a number of distinct (and some less distinct) groups, notably the Sherpas and others such as the Lopas of Mustang.

The Sherpas

The Sherpas are probably the best-known of all the Nepalese ethnic groups for their exploits as mountaineers and Himalayan guides. Before 1950 they were hardly heard of outside the region, but since the first conquest of Everest, they have become famous worldwide, and the name is now synonymous with toughness and cheerfulness.

Their main centres of distribution are in the eastern Himalayan areas of Solu (lowland Sherpas) and Khumbu (the more famous highland Sherpas), though there are Sherpas of varying degrees of similarity established elsewhere in Nepal, e.g. in Helambu. The Solu Sherpas are less distinct, both culturally and ethnically, for they live at a lower altitude and come into contact with a wide range of influences from neighbouring people. The Khumbu Sherpas live in the high altitude area north of Namche Bazaar (Nauche), and are a very distinct group with their own customs and dress. Their origin is in Tibet, and it seems that they came into their present area about 300 to 400 years ago. Their links with Tibet have always remained strong, at least until recently, and much of their dress and customs is similar to that of Tibetans.

The Sherpa way of life involves a mixture of many things, and their whole culture is under pressure from the increasing tourist traffic in Nepal. They are essentially farmers, growing potatoes, buckwheat or barley and keeping flocks of grazing animals, but the climate is harsh in Khumbu, so there are long periods when cultivation is impossible. At this time, in winter, most younger Sherpas leave Khumbu and head for lower areas, including Kathmandu and the Terai, to find other work or to trade. This fits in well with their increasing employment as guides and leaders in trekking and mountaineering expeditions, which normally take place out of the monsoon season, leaving the Sherpas free for the summer to return to Khumbu to work on the land. We have noticed in the last few years, though, a tendency for younger Sherpas to stay on in Kathmandu all the year, mending tents, and doing other preparatory work in the off-season, and the effect on Sherpa homelife may ultimately become significant.

The Sherpa pastoral economy is centred around the yak, those great shaggy beasts that are so familiar in stories of the high Himalayas. They are hardy beasts of burden, providers of milk and milk products, and a source of wool, meat and fuel (from dried dung). They are also a source of income as the Sherpas are skilled breeders, producing valuable yak-cattle hybrids (male Dzopkyos and female Dzums) which combine the virtues of both parents and are in great demand in Tibet and adjacent parts of Nepal. Even this trade has declined, though, owing to the increasing difficulties of dealing with Tibet.

The Sherpas are strongly Buddhist, and Khumbu is one of the most active centres of Tibetan Buddhism in Nepal. Broadly speaking they follow the Ningma-Pa sect of Tibetan Buddhism, and all the Gompas (monasteries) of Khumbu are Ningma-Pa (otherwise known as the Red Hat, or unreformed sect). The Sherpas celebrate several festivals, usually with great gaiety, and these include Lhosar, the Tibetan New Year, when most Sherpas come home to begin work in the fields, some time in February; Dumdze in the middle of summer; and the famous Mani Rimdu ceremonies which attract so many visitors. These latter take place twice a year, in May at Thame and in November at Tengboche. The latter, at Tengboche occurs at the height of the autumn trekking season, and is an exciting and colourful occasion attended by many hundreds of Sherpas as well as many visitors. Tengboche, in the shadow of Everest, and one of the most beautiful places in the world, is the most important monastery in the area because of the presence there of a learned reincarnated Lama (Avatari) as abbot.

Sherpa houses are characteristically built of stone, with two storeys, topped by a shingle roof. The ground floor is used for storage and for the livestock, in a similar way to many alpine houses, while upstairs are the living quarters. These usually consist of one room only, where everybody lives, with a latrine opening into the stables below. A few houses have a little shrine at one end, when they can afford the space.

Marriage arrangements are strict in the sense that people must marry outside their own clan, and must marry inside their own group. Their society is split into a number of clans whose only real function is to prevent interbreeding, though the division of the society into two groups of differing social status has more significance, and individuals are cast out from the higher group (Khadev) if they marry into the lower group (Khamedu). In other respects, their attitude to marriage and sexual relations is free and easy, as some trekkers have been surprised to find. Polygamy occurs occasionally, and we certainly know of Sherpas with wives in both Kathmandu and Khumbu, while polyandry may occur where two brothers are involved.

Sherpa traditional dress is similar to Tibetan dress, and to that of the Lhomi people and others further east. Men wear a long-sleeved heavy coat, the Chuba or Bakkhu, usually worn so that the right shoulder is bare, over a cotton shirt. The coat is often tied by a sash at the waist. The women wear a long shirt, the Ghorma, under a woollen Shyama held by a belt. Over this, they wear the familiar tripartite striped apron. On special occasions, a silk blouse may be worn, more or less hidden by a long, heavy woollen one-piece dress.

Many ornaments are worn, including earrings, necklaces and pendants.

Further east, away from Khumbu, there are other Himalayan people, clearly separated from Sherpas, though probably of similar origin and sharing a number of common characteristics. The Lhomi people of the upper Arun valley are similar in appearance to Sherpas, but they practise more animism and Jhankrism than Buddhism, and their lifestyle is generally simpler. Much further to the west, in Mustang, live the Lopas (Lo is the main district of Mustang) in the high arid trans-Himalayan region with more affinities with Tibet than Nepal. They are of Tibetan origin, and they loosely follow the Sakya-Pa sect of Buddhism. Until recently, they were ruled by a Raja, to whom they paid taxes and for whom they worked, but since 1952 they have been released from this archaic burden.

The 'Bhotias'

As already explained, this is a vague term misleadingly applied to a whole range of people exhibiting Tibetan influence and living near the Tibetan borders. There is, however, a considerable number of people living in the high mountains who are of relatively recent Tibetan origin, only some of whom fall into the category of 'Tibetan refugees'. The high village of Langtang, for instance, in the Langtang National Park, is inhabited mainly by people who came over from Tibet some while ago, certainly several generations. Their language dialect and general cultural affinities indicate that they came from the Kyirong area. They are now well-established as Nepalis, though many of their characteristics are Tibetan. There is a whole range of such peoples, from the recent refugees now all over Nepal (who may or may not be Nepali citizens) to the longer-established groups of known Tibetan origin, such as the Sherpas who are now Nepalese in all respects. Tibetan refugees who have entered Nepal since the 'liberation' of Tibet by Chinese in the 1950s are gradually becoming absorbed into the Nepalese culture, as have so many groups before them. They live in camps and settlements over much of Nepal, particularly in Kathmandu, Pokhara, and the higher valleys. The Tibetans are very active people, and great traders, and wherever they settle they soon start selling their carpets and other handicrafts. They are also noted for running excellent restaurants.

Although their way of life may have changed considerably as they have made use of the opportunities provided by the Nepalese cities, their habits and dress are normally essentially Tibetan, and they are easily recognized, with the exception of some of the young men. The men wear long robes (Chubas) which leave the right shoulder bare, and their hair is long and usually plaited. The traditional multi-coloured felt and leather boots are often worn, and some older Tibetans wear the fur-trimmed caps with ear-covers. The women wear a long gown, folded at the back, and – particularly characteristic – a tripartite striped apron over the top of this.

An attempt has been made to condense the variation and interest of many millions of people into one short chapter, and inevitably much has been left out. We hope, however, that this will give the reader some understanding of the complexity and value of Nepalese society, and some knowledge of the main ethnic and cultural groups to be encountered during a stay in Kathmandu or a trek in the hills.

Religion, Temples and Festivals

For the visitor, uninitiated into the complexities of Hinduism and Buddhism, the enormous profusion of temples and shrines with their countless gods and goddesses, the many small and large festivals occurring throughout the year, and even just the daily religious rituals of the local inhabitants, may leave them baffled and confused.

It *is* confusing. Normally Christians worship in churches, Moslems in mosques, Jews in synagogues, and all worship is directed by their respective priests. But the Nepalese temples are not 'Houses of God' in that sense, confined to one religion. The same temple is visited by both Hindu and Buddhist, and both worship directly to their own gods. Their god may be either Brahma or Buddha, but both are represented in a thousand different forms or incarnations, and different villages, castes and social classes may observe different gods in different ways, while intertwined with these two religions there are still the influences of primitive animistic and Tantric rituals.

This extraordinary and seemingly confused, yet harmonious, state is unique to Nepal, a land of religious tolerance where Buddhism and Hinduism have integrated and interacted, adding to, shaping and colouring one another. To discuss this phenomenon is to describe a way of life. Religion, manifested in its temples, festivals and daily rituals, controls, dictates and provides the meaning and cause of the life of the Nepalese.

The Nepalese believe in the inevitable, that all experience passes from life to death, and that both before and after death they are in constant danger from the evil which is all around them. This evil occurs in the forms of demons, spirits and disease. Their gods represent this evil in what they describe as 'fearful aspects', and they must be constantly worshipped by prayer and animal sacrifice. By doing this the gods will be pleased and look upon them benevolently, in their 'sublime aspect'.

In order to understand just why religion and all its gods, goddesses and rituals plays such an all-important part in the lives of the Nepalese we should look briefly at its development over the centuries.

Hinduism
Nepal is a land of high mountains, rushing rivers and forests full of flowers, mammals, snakes and birds. The ancient Nepalese lived very close to the land and developed the belief that all things have souls, from the smallest pebble to the highest mountain. The spirits in these souls might be good or evil, and if the people were to avoid the natural calamities of disease, death or sterility these spirits had to be worshipped. So developed primitive animistic rituals to guard them against such calamities and many of these beliefs and rituals are still present in Nepal today.

About 1500 BC the Aryan tribes overran the Indian continent bringing with them their own Vedic gods. These gods were nature gods, embodiments of the natural phenomena of Sun, Moon, Earth, Sky, Fire, Water, Sex and Wind. As they spread into India and Nepal so they were absorbed by the indigenous people, who began to worship them alongside their own spirit and demon gods. Some Vedic gods still survive in their own right, such as Surya the Sun god, while others have been assimilated and incorporated into the deities that have since developed.

Associated with these gods, the first system of rituals carried out specifically to ensure that the aims of worship were achieved began. These rituals grew in importance and complexity and the number of gods and goddesses increased. As this happened so there developed a priesthood performing the rites and sacrifices necessary, and interpreting their significance to the ordinary people. This priesthood grew in size and power until it eventually held complete sway over the population.

Between 600 and 300 BC we see the emergence of the Hindu

principle of Brahman, the One, infinite, all-powerful, universal essence. The ultimate goal of all Hindus is to achieve union with Brahman. This is only achieved through constant worship and many reincarnations. Man is born and reborn again, at higher or lower levels, depending on the balance of his good and bad deeds. If he is born at a lower level it may be at a lower caste, or even an untouchable, or an animal. But if he leads a good and saintly life he may eventually reach Brahman.

The Hindu religion has hundreds of deities which can be better understood when we realize that each god is known in many forms. Males, female, or neuter; human, animal or inanimate; benevolent or kind; ferocious or blood-thirsty. It is to these deities that Hindus worship and make offerings asking for protection and assistance in this life and the life after, not only for themselves but for their dead ancestors also. They worship through these deities to the Infinite One, and through their gods they reach the one God. In other words, although it rarely appears so, Hinduism is a religion with one God, in the same way that Christianity, Judaism and Islam are.

Brahman is personified in the Hindu trinity of Brahma, Vishnu and Shiva. Brahma is the mystical absolute manifested so that he can be understood by mortal minds. He is the creator of all things. From his body come the four main castes of Hinduism. The highest caste, the Brahmins, come from his head; the Kshattriya, the ruler-warrior caste, from his arms; the Vaisyas, traders, merchants and landowners, from his legs; the Sudras, servants, labourers and menials, from his feet. Brahma, however, is not a popular god in Nepal, possibly because he is the Absolute, living in refined air and far removed from the practical necessities of day-to-day living, which are the prominent concern of the Nepalese.

Vishnu, on the other hand, is a very popular god, and it is thought that the king is one of his many incarnations. He is the preserver of life, protector of all that has been created. He appears, and is worshipped, under countless manifestations and names. Since the world began, he has, in his capacity as Preserver and Saviour of the World, appeared as an incarnation nine times. These include Rama, Krishna and Narayan, the most popular form of Vishnu in Nepal. Interestingly the ninth incarnation is Buddha.

Shiva is the Destroyer, whose home is on Mount Kailas in Tibet. Unlike Vishnu he has only a few incarnations but many manifestations. One of these is Pashupati, protector of cattle and Lord of the

Earth, and also the tutelary god of Nepal. In his fierce aspect he is represented as Bhairab, of which there are sixty-four forms, all very demonic. But he is also the Regenerator, whose representation is the Lingam, the male phallus. This is the most common idol in the valley of which the lingam at Pashupatinath is the most venerated. It is usually found in conjunction with the Yoni, the female element, a flat disc with a lip opening to one side representing the uterus. No doubt these idols had direct sexual reference at one time, but they are now considered simply as embodiments of Shiva, and represent the philosophical unity of male and female energies, perfect conscious-ness. This is an important element in both Hindu and Buddhist philosophy.

The worship of the female energy is known as Shaktism and it is embodied in the Great Mother Goddesses. These are Shiva's wives: Durga, Kali, Sakti, Parbati, Devi known by many names and appearing in many aspects. The more peaceful mother goddesses, such as the popular goddess Tara, have a place in home worship, but the more terrifying Durga and Kali are very temperamental and need continual appeasement.

Buddhism

Gautama Buddha (or Sakyamuni) was born in Lumbini in 563 BC of a wealthy Kshattriya Raja. He gave up his good life to find the cause and end of suffering. He taught that Nirvana, the state of ultimate awareness, could be reached by strict individual morality combined with mental concentration and wisdom. If anyone followed this law they could break through the wheel of existence, earthly existence, into Nirvana. Both Hindu and Buddhist believe in reincarnation and the accrual of religious merit during their lives so that their next life will be better, but Buddhists do not believe in a single all-powerful deity. They imitate Buddha, rather than worshipping him as an omniscient god.

These teachings were adapted into the everyday lives of the Nepalese who found the gap between themselves and Nirvana difficult to understand. They needed to be able to approach their god on a more personal level. So into the philosophy came the Bhodisattvas, intermediaries between man and Nirvana (said to be men who have turned back from the edge of Nirvana to help their fellow men), thus creating three possible Buddha bodies: the Absolute which is unmanifest; the Bhodisattva; and Human. These were first represented by three Buddhas, each embodying one quality of

Buddhahood: Buddha Vairocana, the embodiment of perfection; on his left, Buddha Akshobhya, symbol of power; on his right, Buddha Amitabha, boundless light. Buddha Sakyamuni continued in his own right as the essence of Buddhahood.

As Hinduism spread through Nepal, so did its influence on Buddhism. Tantricism, with its mystical spells and magical secret rites controlled by a complicated symbolism giving promise of a speedy Nirvana, also began to have a powerful influence on Buddhism. These became integrated into the Buddhist philosophy which adopted many of their ideas and gods, giving them status within its own deities, or creating new ones. From here developed the concept that for the gentle aspect of each Buddha there is a corresponding dreadful aspect. These dreadful aspects represent the five basic human evils: desire, stupidity, wrath, envy and malignity. They are represented in the Mandala, a formalized design of Buddhas, Bhodisattvas and demons which, when used correctly with the appropriate *mantra* or spell, can bring about the desired result.

It was at the level of Bhodisattva that many of the Hindu deities were accepted, and they assumed the gentle or dreadful aspects as needed. Amongst the more important Bhodisattvas are the following: Avalokitesvara – represented in many forms such as Lokesvara, Lord of the World, in which he is synonymous with Shiva. Also as Padmapani ('Lotus in Hand') and Nilakantha, another aspect of Shiva; and Manjusri – famous in the legendary history of Nepal as having cut a way through the mountains, so draining waters of the lake and revealing what is now the Kathmandu valley.

The original doctrine of Gautama Buddha had relied on a celibate priesthood practising the Enlightened Way and teaching it to the laity, but with the advent of Hinduism and the daily contact of the Nepalese with their new Hindu neighbours this priesthood and their monasteries declined.

There has never been any serious conflict between the two religions and both have absorbed the more primitive principles of animism and tantricism. Today they continue to exist in harmony, with their gods as often as not sharing the same temple or temple precincts.

Temples

It is these two religions that have provided the cause and meaning of life for the vast majority of Nepalese. Virtually all the gods and goddesses, myths and legends, motifs and symbols, that have been present in Nepal for centuries belong to these religions.

Both originated in India, though Buddhism went on to Tibet and China and returned at a later date in a different form to add yet another colourful strand in Nepal's religious web. With these religious influences came their respective forms of art and iconography, providing the same sort of subtle, and not so subtle, changes associated with the rituals and worship.

The Emperor Ashoka probably had the greatest influence in terms of religious structures with his deliberate attempts to set up various Buddhist monuments throughout Nepal, such as his stupas in Patan. But more permanent effects occurred later as Nepal developed its trading, cultural and religious contacts with India. Indian artists travelled with the priests, traders and merchants who visited and established themselves in Nepal. Probably they were then employed by local patrons to supply their religious requirements. In so doing they will have undoubtedly apprenticed local Nepalese as wood and stone carvers, metal workers, painters and architects, and gradually an independent, professional artist class developed in Nepal, particularly amongst the Newars, who, since then, have been the most dominant cultural group in Nepal.

It was during the fourth to seventh centuries that the Guptas ruled in India and under them a highly sophisticated culture flourished. At the same time the Licchavis ruled in Nepal and established intimate ties with the Guptas. The consequence was a quite definite influence on the Newars reflected in the art of that period. Another major period of influence was during the eighth and ninth centuries when the new ideology of tantricism was flourishing. It found a ready home in Nepal where magic spells and symbolism already held an important place in its religions. Another important Indian trend of art work appeared during the ninth to twelfth centuries known as the Pala and Sena school of eastern India. In the later half of this period the Malla dynasties emerged in Nepal. As they had originated from this area of India, it was natural that these close links would provide the channels for yet more influence on the Newars. The Malla dynasties also saw the greatest encouragement and growth of all forms of art in Nepal.

Virtually all art in Nepal is of a religious nature, and virtually all of it is found in, on, or around its temples.

The most typical Nepalese religious architectural form is that of the pagoda. It stands on a square base, or plinth, and is built of brick and wood with a number of roofs, ranging from two to five, rising upwards like a tower in receding tiers. The ground floor is the most important, housing the deity, while the upper levels serve no real function now, but add considerably to the whole aesthetic appeal of the temple. These receding tiers are considered by some experts to represent the umbrellas that protect the deity from the elements, or perhaps that they are a representation of the umbrellas that are carried to protect the Nepalese kings themselves from the elements. For it was during the reign of the Malla dynasties, in particular during the seventeenth and eighteenth centuries, that the pagoda form first appeared and developed fully. It was with the king's encouragement and funds that these temples were built, particularly around the Durbar squares, adjacent to their palaces, and it was in Nepal that the pagoda style is thought to have originated.

The most interesting feature of these temples is often their woodwork, including beautifully carved eaves, lintels, doors, panels, windows and struts which seem to support the whole weight of the slanting roofs. Most of these decorative carvings are symbolic icons of the various deities, from the simple relief of a goddess to three-dimensional pieces depicting gods with many arms, and lion-like beasts of protection.

One particular feature of wood carving found on these supporting struts that is liable to generate particular interest is that of eroticism. The original meaning of these carvings is not clearly known, but we can assume that they have their origins in the primitive religions of the Nepalese. Then procreation was an essential element in the battle for survival. It was no more important perhaps than death, or family, or ploughing the fields, but another integral part of the structure of life. The Aryans, with their Vedic gods and goddesses, viewed the sexual act as part of the whole web of life and possibly this is how it survived. If we look at all the representations the Newar craftsmen have shown in their temples, then eroticism is but a small part, but equal with the other elements of life, earthly or otherwise. Nevertheless, for those who are unused to this frank approach to one essential element of life, the depiction of a variety of sexual acts on the structures of a temple may come as a shock initially.

Another aspect of wood carving that the Newars seem to have excelled in is that of their windows. Beautiful examples can be found everywhere, not just on the temples, but also on their houses. One example is that of a peacock with the body as the centre piece, while the tail radiates outwards to give an incredible latticed design.

Another is of Surya surrounded by a circle of human skulls, and yet another is of Krishna flirting with some shepherdesses.

The doorways that lead to the inner sanctum are known as Torana, of which the most outstanding example in Nepal, and perhaps the Buddhist and Hindu world, is that of the Golden Gate in Bhadgaon. On these doorways are embellished, in carved wood and beaten brass, figures of the various deities, flowers, animals and demons. They serve to enhance and protect the shrine. Commonly found in front of these doorways are the Dvarpals, or the deity guards, which are usually depicted as fierce dragons or man lions.

Shikaras are another form of temple that are an essentially Indian design. There is considerable variation in this form, from the simple tower to the elaborately decorated and multi-towered versions, such as the Krishna Mandir temple in Patan. In this form the temple is built almost entirely of bricks and mortar. Constructed on a square plinth, similar to that of the pagodas, it rises up as a square tower for about half its height, when it curves inwards to culminate near the top in the shape of a flower vase. At the base, a small room houses the god or goddesses for which the temple was erected. This form can become more elaborate with the addition of pillars, balconies and surrounding but connected towers, so that the final shikara may contain many storeys and house an army of deities.

Both the pagoda and the shikara house Buddhist and Hindu deities, and consequently both religious groups worship at these temples. The stupa, however, is exclusively Buddhist, of which the oldest in Nepal are said to be the Ashoka stupas of Patan. The most famous of the Buddhist stupas are those of Swayambunath and Bodnath.

The base usually consists of a stepped pyramidal platform. On this rests a semi-global dome surmounted by a large square tower, the haimika. On all four sides of this tower are a pair of 'all-seeing eyes'. At the Bodnath stupa the base is in the shape of a mandala, representing the world. There are thirteen steps between the dome and the tower, said to represent the thirteen stages one must progress through to reach Bhodi, perfect knowledge. Around this structure can usually be found a wall housing a number of prayer wheels and the four cardinal Buddhas.

The highest concentration of temples are to be found in the Durbar squares of Kathmandu, Patan and Bhadgaon, though rarely will these temple areas be exclusively either Buddhist or Hindu. Others can be found at important sites away from the cities and villages, such as Swayambunath, Changu Narayan, Dakshinkali, and yet others may be found almost anywhere, in a field, on top of a pass, or in the middle of a small wood. In each town the various wards or toles will each have their own squares containing their own particular deities along with a number of associate, subordinate and attendant deities. These, and those installed in private houses, are the ones that are worshipped and propitiated daily.

Festivals

As we mentioned at the beginning of this section, religion is a way of life in Nepal. We see it in the degupuja, the daily worship the Nepalese offer to their ancestors and a host of other deities, and in the innumerable colourful and exciting festivals that occur throughout the year. These are celebrated in all parts of Nepal, but it is in the Kathmandu valley that the most numerous, elaborate and most colourful occur.

These festivals occur regularly on specific days of the lunar calendar and therefore vary slightly in each year of our own calendar. Also, as we mentioned before, original interpretations and method of celebration vary with the caste, social class and religion of those involved, though the basic purposes are the same.

The whole structure of Nepalese society is based on the closeknit extended family unit, with several generations living in one household. Particular reverence is paid to the mother and father, though brothers and sisters are always worshipped at some point during the year. This structure is maintained through various religious teachings and numerous festivals and ceremonies designed specifically to foster and enhance such close family bonds.

Ancestor worship is a natural and integral part of the daily life of the Nepalese. The first priority in the morning, after washing which ritually purifies the body, is to offer food and water to the souls of the dead. These rituals bring sustenance and comfort and also reincarnation at a higher level for the dead, while giving great religious merit to the actual worshipper. In many homes ancestors are deified as household gods who, if worshipped, will protect the household, but, who, if neglected, will appear as ghosts to haunt the household members.

For up to one year after cremation or burial the dead person's soul wanders aimlessly awaiting entrance to the Underworld. It is the inescapable duty of those living relatives to see that the soul is provided with enough food and comfort until it passes through the

Judgement Gates. This involves degupuja and certain well-defined pujas in various festivals and ceremonies, and includes the donation of large amounts of food, clothing and money to priests who accept these offerings on behalf of the deceased.

Yama Raj, the God of Death, lives in the Underworld where he keeps a great ledger in which is recorded every human being's birth, their good and bad deeds in their various lives, and the predetermined date of their death in each life. When their death is due Yama Raj sends a black crow to collect them and put them on the path to the Judgement Gates. This path is liable to be long, arduous and extremely dangerous, and it is the hope of the living relatives that in their pujas they will be able to call on the Holy Cow to act as a guide through these ordeals. The soul of the deceased will hold on to the tail of the Holy Cow until they reach the Judgement Gates, when she will push them open with her great horns. The Gai Jatra festival, during August–September, is the occasion when the Holy Cow is venerated and thanked for her help in such an important stage in the soul's search for peace. When one realizes that most Nepalese believe that the date of their death is predetermined, it helps to explain the bravery and even recklessness of their soldiers, drivers and others!

Numerous other family festivals occur throughout the year, and these give some insight into the extended family's commitments to ancestor worship, of which elements can be found in all the festivals of Nepal, though other festivals may serve a much larger purpose. A few examples of the more important general festivals that occur throughout the year are as follows.

The festival of Red Machendranath (April–May) is one of the most spectacular of the valley's festivals, celebrated in Patan by thousands of participants, particularly amongst the Newars. Machendranath is worshipped by Hindus as saint Machendra himself, or as Karaunamaya, the compassionate god of mercy. Buddhists worship him as an incarnation of Lokeswar, Lord of the World. He is also known by many in the valley as Bunga Deo, god of Bunga. Initial ceremonies start two weeks before the big procession at Lagankhel, where the image is taken to be bathed in holy water. Thousands of excited devotees jostle to see the rites performed. The image is then taken away and repainted, and several important rituals occur. As soon as these are completed, he is taken and placed in his chariot at Phulchowk. Here, thousands of worshippers have been singing, praying and chanting for days while work goes on building the chariot temple. This chariot is a swaying spire of bamboo struts, covered in evergreen branches, and supported on four enormous wheels which represent four Bhairab deities. Four days later, he moves off, followed by a similar though less unwieldy chariot, housing the idol of Min Nath, or Chakuwa Dev, considered to be Machendra's daughter (or son!).

The festival really moves into full swing now as the chariots sway down narrow streets surrounded by thousands of worshippers. Military bands and local musicians provide a constant barrage of noise, only surpassed by the roar from the near-ecstatic crowds themselves. Hundreds pull and tug at the ropes, dragging the chariots through the streets, and old Newari ladies and very young children, in special costumes for the occasion, walk alongside the mobile though decidedly unwieldy temples. The chariots stop at predetermined places, where the local inhabitants rush out to throw offerings over the idols and touch the wheels of the Bhairabs and the long wooden yoke that represents the snake god. Animals are sacrificed to pacify the Bhairabs. When the chariots reach Lagan-khel, they circle the pipal tree, which represents Machendra's mother, three times. There is a favourite story which tells that the women of Pode Tole sleep without clothes the night Machendra stops there, in the hope that he might visit them. We have not been able to confirm this. The climax of the celebrations occurs when the 'bhoto' is shown, which may happen any time between May and September, depending on the astrologers' interpretations of the stars. In 1976, it finished in mid-September.

The story tells that Karkot Naga, the snake god, once gave a splendid jewel-encrusted waistcoat (the bhoto) to an eye-healer who had healed a sore on the eye of his serpent queen (in other versions, a wise man cured the dangerously sick queen). Unfortunately, the healer had the bhoto stolen. Some years later, during the Machendranath festival, he spotted the thief wearing his bhoto, and naturally a great argument ensued. Karkot Naga decided the problem finally by donating it to Lord Machendra, and each year it is shown from the chariot to the excited crowds below.

On this occasion, the Kumari of Patan is taken to witness the showing, and receives no small amount of adulation herself. The king and queen of Nepal, top-ranking government officials and military officers also came to see the bhoto, and pay their respects to Machendranath. Inevitably some rain will fall on that day as Machendra thanks them for their devotions. One important ritual has to be performed before Machendra returns to his temple in

Patan, and it is awaited in tense expectation by the thousands gathered there. A priest climbs to the top of the spire and drops a copper bowl-shaped disc. If it falls face down, then all is well, but if it falls face upwards, mouth open to the skies, this means that the following year may see the people suffering from hunger.

The festival of Indra Jatra in September–October in legend symbolizes the mortification of the people of the valley who accidentally took Lord Indra (ruler of Heaven) prisoner when he appeared in human form. A few days before the official start of the ceremonies a 50-foot tree, representing Shiva's lingam, is cut from the forest of Yosingu near Bhadgaon. It is then sanctified by the royal priests with animal sacrifices and dragged in various stages to Hanuman Dhoka in Kathmandu. The moment for its raising is decided by the astrologers, and surrounded by thousands of people, numerous military and local bands in friendly rivalry and the roar of canons on the Tundikhel, it is hauled upright. At its base is placed an image of Indra and his carrier the elephant, and from the top Indra's flag is unfurled. The ceremonies begin.

As soon as this has happened, all over Kathmandu images of the bound Indra and masks of the Blue Bhairab are placed out in the streets under elaborately decorated canopies. At dusk hundreds of people in whose family a death occurred during the last year walk the streets making offerings to these images. In Durbar square all the temples are lit by thousands of small oil lamps and exotically masked dancers whirl in a frenzy of dances that depict the ten incarnations of Vishnu.

The chariot ride of the Living Goddess, Kumari, appears to have been instituted during the reign of King Jaya Prakash Malla. One story runs that a young Newar girl became possessed by the spirit of Taleju, the divine Mother Goddess, who for centuries has been the patron deity of Nepal and her royal families. The king, thinking that she was a fraud, banished her, but that same night one of his queens became possessed and said that the spirit of Taleju had now entered her. The king rapidly recalled the girl, publicly proclaimed her to be Kumari, and worshipped at her feet. He built her a new home and ordained that there be an annual chariot ride in her honour.

Another legend suggests that the king lusted after the beautiful Taleju, who promptly told him that his dynasty would fall (which it did shortly afterwards), and that from that time he was to worship her through a young Newar girl, but there are other versions too.

The Kumari is selected from the Newar Sakya (goldsmith) caste, a Buddhist caste, usually when she is about three years old. She must have an unblemished skin, have lost no teeth and not have bled in any way. Though the selection rites are secret, it is thought that she is led into a darkened room where the severed heads of animals litter the floor. Priests in weird and frightening masks leap out at her with terrifying screams. If she shows no fear then she is selected as the next Kumari. Her attendants, two young boys representing Ganesh and Bhairab, are thought to be selected in the same way.

There are said to be eleven Kumaris in the valley, but the Kathmandu Kumari is by far the most important. It is her job to 'advise' the local people and the royal family alike, and to attend certain ceremonies throughout the year. During Indra Jatra she symbolically bestows upon the king the right to rule for another year by placing the red tika mark on his forehead. The king traditionally thanks her with a golden coin and by touching her feet with his forehead.

At the first shedding of blood the Kumari is immediately replaced by another young girl. It is said that ex-Kumaris find it difficult to marry as the man who ends her virginity dies shortly afterwards, while others will ask what is the use of a wife who knows nothing of motherhood, housekeeping or cooking! The last Kumari is still happily married, however, with her husband alive and well!

Before the house of Kumari, the square is solid with thousands of people waiting to see the goddess emerge. Foreign and Nepalese dignitaries line the balcony of the old palace finally joined by the king and queen of Nepal. Bands play, dancers reel and the whole atmosphere of expectancy and excitement is overwhelming. When the Kumari appears the hysterical crowds roar their approval and surge forward to touch the goddess. Her helpers have to beat back the worshippers as they are in great danger of being crushed and suffocated. The watching visitor cannot help but be stunned at the great waves of adoration that pour from the crowd over this small, quiet girl.

Shortly afterwards Ganesh and Bhairab appear. Military guns fire a salute and the chariots move off. They pause beneath the balcony where the king bows to the little goddess. The already hysterical crowd roar their approval and can only be described as in a state of organized riot! The chariots then move off to circuit the streets of the old city.

It was on this day in 1768 that Prithwi Narayan Shah entered Kathmandu. Jaya Prakash Malla, unable to raise his troops from the intoxicated crowds, fled in defeat to Patan, just as Taleju had prophesied. The festival continued and Kumari gave her blessing instead to Prithwi and so the reign of the Shah kings started!

Dasain or Durga Puja in September–October is the longest, most festive and most auspicious festival celebrated throughout the country. For nearly two weeks, families are reunited, pageants are held and the goddess Durga, in her many forms and manifestations, is venerated with thousands and thousands of animal sacrifices.

All of Nepal's military, educational and political institutions come to a standstill, and, along with the major business houses, are closed for ten to fifteen days. From all over the country and other parts of the world family members travel to the homes of their mothers and fathers. Shops do a brisk business as presents are bought and into the valley are herded hundreds of buffaloes, goats and sheep.

Dasain is a major festival, celebrated throughout the Hindu world as the time when the god Rama overcame Ravana, the king of the evil demon hordes, thus freeing the people from fear. Although it is based on the Ramayana epic, it has, of course, become modified and adapted in Nepal, and the divine goddess Durga is worshipped for her slaying of the demon Mahisasura in the form of a ferocious water buffalo.

The first nine days are known as Nawa Ratri (Nine Nights) and are devoted to the worship of Shakti, the energy and power of the female, depicted as Durga in nine different aspects. During each of these nights devotees must bathe at different sacred spots, and before dawn each morning present offerings to the temples of Durga. These contain a variety of forms of Durga such as the simple kalash, or water jug, or as the Great Protectress, who controls the mysteries of life and death, birth, procreation and fertility, with eighteen hands all holding a murderous weapon. Then again as Kali, the Destructress, wearing a necklace of skulls, her tongue dripping with blood and standing on the mangled corpses of her victims.

On the first day of Dasain, Ghatasthapana, a kalash (water jug) is placed in a purified and blessed room of the house. It is filled with holy water and decorated on the outside with cow dung, considered in Nepal to be a purifying element. In the dung are planted barley seeds. At just the right moment, once again determined by the astrologers, a puja is performed and the vessel is believed to have become the actual goddess, Durga. Each day it is blessed with a sprinkling of holy water, and ceremonial rituals are performed around it constantly during the ten days. During the last few days of Dasain, parents put barley shoots into the hair of their sons and daughters as a blessing from them and the goddess.

The seventh day is known as Fulpati, the day of sacred flowers and leaves, when the sacred kalash of the royal family is installed in the old palace of Hanuman Dhoka. This kalash is carried from the ancestral palace in Gurkha by royal Brahmin priests. They arrive in Kathmandu on the third day, where hundreds of government officials wait to receive them at Rani Pokhari. As the kalash arrives, the military cannon boom out a welcome. As this is happening, the king and queen are reviewing the troops and receiving foreign dignitaries on the Tundhikel parade ground. Meanwhile, the kalash is carried through the masses to the inner chambers of Hanuman Dhoka where, shortly afterwards, the king and queen will arrive to worship it. The eighth night is known as Kalratri or black night, when thousands of animal sacrifices take place in temples through-out the country. On the following day, many more sacrifices take place as military leaders and many others ask Durga for protection during the coming year. Those animals that are sacrificed are thought by the Nepalese to be relieved of their burdens of animal bodies to be reincarnated later in human bodies, so the acts do not seem cruel to them.

The tenth day, Vijaya Dashami, is the day that Durga (and Rama) appeared riding a lion to slay the ferocious Mahisasura (or Ravana) in response to the pleadings and prayers of gods and men, and marks the official conclusion of Dasain, and is the height of the celebration.

It is obligatory on this day for all Hindus to visit all their elder relatives and superiors in order of seniority or rank, starting with their parents. The purpose is to receive the Tika blessing, an ancient symbol of victory and power and now worn as a token of good fortune and decoration. This day the king receives senior members of parliament, military officers and representatives of the general public, and bestows upon them the Tika blessing.

The holy kalash in the homes are dismantled in religious rituals, and the priests ask Durga for her protection and peace. Nepal gradually returns to normal, convinced that all its efforts in the last ten days will ensure that the people are safe from harm and misery during the following year.

One of the many advantages of visiting Nepal in the autumn is the number and variety of festivals that take place after harvest is gathered in. Barely two weeks after Dasain, with life only just back to normal, the great colourful festival of Tihar or Diwali (October –November) begins. For those who find the blood and sacrifices of

Dasain horrific, this is perhaps the most attractive of Nepal's festivals, with its colourful garlands of flowers and general air of bonhomie.

Tihar lasts for five days. The first day is dedicated to crows, which are worshipped as the messengers of Yama by the spreading of rice-grains at convenient points.

The second day is dogs' day. Dogs (unlike cats, which are unpopular) are common throughout the valley and the rest of Nepal, and they are worshipped both for their religious significance and for their faithful qualities as companions and guardians. On dogs' day, the lucky dogs are fed special food, garlanded with flowers, and even decorated with flowers, though the significance of all this may well be lost on them!

On the third day, at least in the morning, cows are worshipped. Cows have assumed great significance in the Hindu religion for many centuries, probably since the Aryan tribes used them to help them across the desert on the way to India, and now they are believed to push open the doors of heaven when the dead come to enter. Like the dogs on their day, the cows are garlanded, decorated and feasted on their great day. Then, in the afternoon of the third day, preparations are made for the visit of the goddess Lakshmi, the goddess of wealth, and lights pop up all over the city to show her the way to houses where she is welcome, for she will not visit ill-prepared homes.

On the fourth day, oxen and bullocks are worshipped, and one's own body is honoured for the divine spirit within it.

The fifth day is brother-sister day, and also the Newar New Year. On this day brothers visit their sisters and ply them with gifts while the sisters bestow garlands, prayers and cooked delicacies on the brother (or a friend if there is no brother). This celebrates an occasion in the distant past when a girl pleaded so eloquently with Yama for her young brother to be spared from an early death that Yama relented and allowed the boy to live. Tihar ends with family reunions and New Year celebrations amongst the Newars.

There are many more festivals that we have not mentioned, such as Holi, Buddha's birthday, the Tibetan New Year and many more, for there is almost always one or other festival going on somewhere in the country!

5. Nepal's Natural History

Almost every visitor to Nepal becomes interested in the natural history they see there. Whether it is because of the tigers and rhinos of Chitwan, the kites of Kathmandu, the incredible rhododendron forests of the mountains in spring, or simply the sheer variety of it all, you just can't avoid taking an interest. Most sub-tropical countries have a great variety of plants and animals, but Nepal, with the greatest altitude range in the world, has some of everything from sub-tropical through to arctic and alpine in an area of only 54,000 square miles. It is also a historical meeting ground, where the ranges of different types of plants and animals meet and overlap. East Asian or Chinese meets west Asian, and even Mediterranean, while south Asian or Indian meets north Asian, or Tibetan and Siberian.

Between the plains and the mountains, as the altitude increases, the forest changes constantly from deciduous tropical, such as sal forest, up through bands of different oaks, bamboo thickets, and sometimes pure rhododendron forest up to the zone of conifers where spruces, firs, hemlocks and pines predominate. Above these, at the highest forest levels, there are junipers and birch to about 14,000 feet from where scrub and eventually scattered alpines take over. The forests determine everything else, so it is worthwhile following the changes. Each forest type has its typical birds, many ground flowers grow only with specific trees, and many mammals will most often be found in a particular favourite type of forest. Scattered amongst the original forest are the cultivated areas, great tiers of terraces, reaching, it sometimes seems, up to the sky, and dotted with houses and villages where there are cosmopolitan weeds, and cosmopolitan birds, like the House Sparrow.

It is impossible to detail the whole range of Nepal's natural history here, so we have tried instead to explain some of the background, and pick out some of the highlights. There is still much to be discovered, and very few books to help show the way. While in Kathmandu, it is well worth visiting the natural history museum, the botanic gardens at Godavari, and the zoo to see some of the rich variety of life, and to help with identifications.

Plant Life

Within the boundaries of Nepal, there are an estimated 6000 species of plants, from jungle trees to dwarf alpines. There are over forty species of rhododendrons, over 200 species of orchids, and innumerable other attractive flowers. So, we will not be attempting a full description of Nepal's flowers, but rather picking out some of the main features and highlights.

In the Terai, where original vegetation still exists, it is mostly jungle, consisting of sal trees. The economically valuable sal is a rather thin tree, not very tall, and forming open forests with plenty of light, but surprisingly few flowers below. Its lower branches are often cut for fodder. In other areas, where there is no sal, a variety of different trees appear, the most conspicuous of which is the Cotton Silk tree, or Simal, whose bright orange-red blossoms can be seen covering the trees in February, when little else is in flower.

Around the larger midland towns, such as Pokhara and Kathmandu, at 3000 to 4000 feet, there is very little original vegetation left, though there are plenty of plants to see. Perhaps the most conspicuous features are the giant trees planted for shade, and as symbols, at chautharas (resting-places) and shrines. These are the banyan tree (*Ficus benghalensis*), with its trailing aerial roots, and the pipal (*Ficus religiosa*). Both are members of the fig and mulberry family, and are common everywhere through the lowlands. Though Indian in origin, they are very much a part of Nepalese life. Around Pokhara, in particular, there are large bushes, fifteen to twenty feet high, of poinsettias, the same as we grow at home as a small pot plant, but flourishing here in ideal conditions, although its origins are in tropical Mexico. The spiny, almost cactus-like shrub with bright red flowers growing on banks and mud walls is the Crown-of-Thorns spurge from Madagascar, and the trailing creeper often covering whole trees with a mass of purple-bracted flowers is a bougainvillaea, from Brazil.

Along the streets, many different trees are planted. Despite the wealth of native trees, these are nearly all foreign to Nepal. The reason for this odd predominance of exotic plants in Nepalese cities lies in the interest of the Ranas in introducing strange plants to their gardens, and subsequently – on a more local scale – in the introduction made by Gurkhas returning home from the tropics. Along many streets, especially in the Kathmandu valley, the Australian Bottle Brush tree is planted. Its dark green weeping branches bear masses of striking red flowers, frequently surrounded by bees and butterflies, looking remarkably like exotic red bottle brushes. Another striking tree, up to fifty feet high, is the Brazilian jacaranda with finely cut greyish leaves and masses of blue-purple flowers. Other Australian trees planted along the streets include the Silk oak (*Grevillea robusta*) with its silky leaves and clusters of orange flowers, and several species of eucalyptus. Commonly planted shrubs include the Cape jasmine, or gardenia, with its beautifully fragrant large white flowers, the Chinese wisteria with its silvery-grey leaves and spikes of bluish flowers, and great masses of yellow or white jasmine spreading over shrubs and walls alike. Look out, too, for the trailing morning glory with its large, bright blue saucer flowers. On waste ground, one may frequently see strands of hemp (cannabis) growing wild!

Leaving Kathmandu or Pokhara, and trekking or driving north, one soon comes into contact with the hill vegetation. On the lower slopes of the hills, at 3000 to 5000 feet both to the south and north of the valleys, various types of sub-tropical deciduous and evergreen forests occur, rich in all forms of life. When undisturbed, it is often very dense, with creepers, vines and a thick shrub layer. There are too many plants to mention in detail, but it is worth looking out for the beautiful red-flowered Tree rhododendron, camellias, walnuts, a few magnolias, and the very attractive evergreen, creamy-white flowered schima trees which are often dominant over wide areas. It is not surprising that the Tree rhododendron (*Rhododendron arboreum*) is Nepal's national flower. In spring its bushes, or even trees up to seventy feet, are a mass of red flowers, in superb contrast to the blue of the sky and the white of the mountains. It may be found over most of the country from the sub-tropical areas right up to the high forests. Strangely, though, the flower colour gets lighter and lighter with the increasing altitude, and it often lookes like quite a different plant at 10,000 feet. It is one of the first of the rhododendrons to flower, in March and April, and is followed through the early summer by many other species in all their different shades of pink, red and even yellow.

Higher up into the hills, or further into the mountains, in many areas the forest becomes strangely familiar to European and North American eyes. The climate of this zone resembles that of the temperate northern hemisphere, and the predominant trees are often oaks of several different species. The similarity does not bear too close a scrutiny, though. On the ground and along the tree branches, there are many exotic orchids with beautiful huge white, red, purple or yellow flowers. This altitude, from about 8000 to 10,000 feet, is probably the best area for orchids, and amongst them should be mentioned: *Pleiones* – dwarf ground-living orchids with large white and mauve flowers, or on trees, with pink flowers. They are mostly autumn flowers and are strangely specific to altitude e.g. *Pleione praecox* – purple, ground-living, at 7200 to 7600 feet; *Pleione hookeriana*, pink, on trees at about 8800 feet, etc. Blue or rose *Vandas* occur on trees or mossy rocks along with green, yellow or white *Cymbidiums*, long white gracefully drooping racemes of *Coelogyne*, and numerous *Dendrobiums*.

In many areas, there are forests of magnolias and rhododendrons at this height, and in spring they are a superb sight, as, for example, around Tragshindu monastery near the Dudh Kosi, on the Everest trek. In autumn and winter they are mysterious dark places, with the strange shapes of the contorted trunks, and the long streamers of mosses and lichens.

Although conifers, such as the green and beautifully aromatic Chir pine, do occur at much lower altitudes, as at Dhunche near the Langtang valley, they really come into their own at the higher altitudes. Above the oaks, usually at around 10,000 feet, there is often an area of hemlock forest (*Tsuga dumosa*) recognizable by its soft broad needles, often of irregular length. This gives way to the beautiful Silver fir forest, one of the most beautiful of all the forest types. The trees often grow, straight-stemmed, to well over 100 feet, and the branches are covered with erect candle-like cones, while the forest floor below is a mass of rhododendrons, primulas, and shrubby pink and white flowered daphnes and viburnums. In some areas, especially where the forest has been disturbed, there are great thickets of bamboos. Higher still, there is birch forest, as around Tengboche monastery or in the upper Langtang valley. The species is *Betula utilis*, and it is noticeable for its beautiful silvery-brown peeling bark, and the great grey streamers of lichen (*Usnea longissima*) that hang from its branches. Below the trees there are many rhododendrons, and the forest is the favourite haunt of Musk deer. Often the birch forms the limit of the treeline, though in many places gnarled old junipers, with their resinous aroma and berry-like cones, carry on up the slopes. Among other conifers to be seen are the Blue pine with its large bluish cones, the Himalayan or Deodar cedar in the west of the country, and deciduous larch (*Larix griffithii*) in a few areas, such as Langtang.

Above the trees, at about 12,000 feet, and amongst the highest forest where there has been clearance, there are alpine meadows. Most of the glories of these high pastures are missed by the average visitor. In autumn and early winter they are brown and dry, while in winter and early spring they are usually under snow. But from April onwards, as the snow recedes, the pastures spring into life. At first, just patches of dwarf blue iris (*Iris kumaonensis*) appear, followed by the early mauve and pink primulas, often growing through the snow. Then, as summer comes on, the pastures become a mass of irises, primulas, gentians, and golden potentillas, while amongst the rocks there are saxifrages, fritillaries and dozens of other high altitude flowers, seen at their best in July and August.

On the other side of the Himalayas, you might easily be in another country. The whole feel of the place is Tibetan, and the lack of rain here causes a completely different vegetation, more like high-altitude Afghanistan or Chitral. The slopes are bare and inhospit-able, dotted with spiny shrubs, cushion plants and junipers, all able to withstand grazing, cold winds and droughts. The only place the traveller is likely to see this very different vegetation at present is on the recently reopened trek to Muktinath where the trail goes along the great Kali Gandaki. As you pass through the Himalayan wall, all the changes we have described take place, from semi-tropical forest on the southern slopes to semi-desert on the dry northern side, behind the barrier of Annapurna and Dhaulgiri.

Animal Life

Nepal is not only rich in plants. Not surprisingly, in view of the great variety of climates and vegetation types, it is also rich in animal life. Although there are not the teeming variety of numbers of, say, the African game reserves, there is a wealth of different species spread over the country, including a number of particularly interesting or spectacular ones. Richest of all the areas is undoubtedly the Terai, and *the* place to see animals here is in the Chitwan National Park. Casual wandering in such an area would be ill-advised, but luckily there is the opportunity to see most of the life that the area has to offer on an organized tour, by foot and elephant. Chitwan contains one of the world's last remaining populations of the Indian one-horned rhinoceros (as depicted on some Nepalese bank notes). They live amongst the tall 'elephant grass' in the valleys, and an encounter with one of these huge beasts is a memorable experience, particularly as they have a habit of charging you if you get too close! There is also a good population of tigers, recently estimated at thirty, a tenth of those left in the world, and there is always a fair chance of seeing them, as they are regularly encouraged to come to certain areas of the park, while remaining wild.

Amongst other rarer animals are the Gaur bison, the largest ox in the world, an impressive beast sometimes exceeding a height of six feet at the shoulder, and the freshwater Gangetic dolphin which still occurs in the Naryani river, though now exceedingly rare throughout the Ganges. It is surprising enough to learn of dolphins in Nepal, but perhaps even more surprising to learn that there are two species of crocodile to be found in several lowland stretches of Nepal's rivers, including some in Chitwan. There is the incredible Gharial, with its long snout-like nose, and the rather less pleasant Mugger. The Gharial, although sometimes as long as twenty feet, feeds mainly on fish, and is little danger to humans. The Mugger, though, has a rather worse reputation. Both are reptiles, not mammals. Other animals that one might easily see in Chitwan include various deer, such as the Elk-like Sambar, the beautiful Chital, or spotted deer, and the aptly named Hog deer. One other mammal should be mentioned before leaving Chitwan. This is the Termite-eating Sloth bear, possibly the most dangerous animal in Nepal. It has poor sight and hearing, since it has – presumably – no natural enemies to worry about. Consequently, now and again, it is easy to approach a Sloth bear upwind and come upon it unawares. If disturbed in this way, it will often panic and lash out wildly, and cause considerable wounds. It is the only bear in the Nepalese lowlands.

Elsewhere in the Terai, there are small isolated areas containing pockets of other rare mammals. The best of these areas are covered in three wildlife reserves. Sukla Phanta, a beautiful area of about 60 square miles in the western Terai, was established to preserve the only population of Swamp deer in Nepal, though there are also good numbers of Nilgai (Blue Bull), leopard, tiger, Sambar, etc. A small population of wild Water buffalo still live, precariously hanging on, in the Tappu reserve in the eastern Terai around the Kosi river. They are magnificent beasts with very long horns, so different to the scraggy domestic beasts. Recently, a small number of Blackbuck, basically an Indian desert animal, has been rediscovered in the

Terai. They were thought to have been extinct in Nepal for some years prior to this.

The Siwaliks and Mahabharat hills have no particular mammals associated solely with them, but a number of both Terai and Himalayan species are found in the dense forests that grow on the higher slopes. Leopard, bear, various deer, wild boar and various monkeys, for instance, occur throughout the region in suitable habitats. In the Kathmandu valley, the most obvious wild animals are the Rhesus Macaque monkeys, particularly around Swyambunath. Their association with the Hindu religion gives them some protection, though they are a menace to crops at times. The Jungle cat, probably the commonest of the ten or so wild cats in Nepal, will venture into the outskirts of Kathmandu at night, so watch out for a small tawny coloured cat with black rings on its tail. Other animals occasionally seen in the valley include mongoose and jackals, and a sight well worth going to see is the colony of Flying Foxes or Giant Fruit bats which roost during the day in several trees around the Royal Palace area. They disperse in the evening to feed on fruits and flowers (for which they are often the main pollinators): they are said to like mangoes in particular (and who can blame them!). In the forests or protected areas close to Kathmandu, such as Gokarna, there are still leopards and other cats, and various deer, though you would be lucky to see any.

Many people walk for several weeks in the mountains, and never get a glimpse of a mammal. There are a lot there, though, and the early morning walker, or one on a quiet trail, has a very good chance of seeing something. The most frequently seen mammals are the beautiful Langur monkeys, with their grey and white fur, and black faces. They travel in troupes of ten to twenty animals, with quite a strict social organization, and can be seen right up to the forest limit and sometimes beyond. Their agility is amazing, and it is a marvellous sight to watch an adult, often carrying a baby, jump twenty feet or more from rock to rock. Another commonly seen animal, from 6000 to 10,000 feet, is the Himalayan squirrel, inhabiting, as one might expect, the forests around this height. The Flying squirrels, though not rare, are rarely seen because of their largely nocturnal way of life. The Yellow-throated marten is quite often seen in forests right up to the tree limit. It is active in the day, and may be quite tame and apparently fearless. The forests at around 8000 to 10,000 feet are amongst the richest areas for mammals, in terms of numbers, though the dense nature of the vegetation and the fact that people keep to well-defined trails (Nepal's 'motorways'!) means that few of the animals are ever seen. Given luck, or patience, it is quite possible to come across leopard, Black bear, Brown goral (a rather small type of goat-antelope), Barking deer (especially in the late afternoon or evening, when it emerges from its daytime resting-place), Wild boar, and even the Red panda. The last is a beautiful racoon-like animal, one of only two panda species in the world, the other, of course, being the Giant panda of China and zoo fame. It is normally nocturnal, but is occasionally seen in the day, sometimes at very close range, probably when it has been disturbed from its normal daytime hiding-place. It is worth going out into the forest at night and sitting quietly, preferably with a torch ready, to see what is about. The upper zones of the forests are quiet places at night, unlike tropical forests, and it is easy enough to pick out the sounds – such as the short bark of the Barking deer, usually signifying that a leopard is nearby, the chattering of a squirrel, or the hunting call of a passing owl.

In the higher forests and lower meadows (10,000 to 13,000 feet), various other mammals are to be seen in addition to some of those already mentioned. Without doubt the commonest of these is the Pika or Mouse hare. These little, almost hamster-like animals are relatives of the rabbits and hares, and should not be confused with the marmots, which are rodents. Pikas live in the bare rocky areas in great numbers, and they are readily seen though rarely for long, unless you have time to stand and watch quietly. Several times we have had close views of them while answering the calls of nature! The only marmot to be found in Nepal is the Bobak marmot, the same one that occurs right across Asia to Europe, though it is present only in a few isolated mountain areas within Nepal. The high birch forests are the main home of the rare and shy Musk deer. This odd animal has a rather 'hunched' appearance, and two exceptionally long canine teeth, though it suffers from having an extremely valuable musk gland for which it is mercilessly hunted. The musk is valued, by the Chinese in particular, as a potent aphrodisiac (probably wrongly) and pods are said to fetch £1000 or more, so there is little wonder that it has become a much rarer species in recent years. It is now the subject of intensive study, before pressure from hunters reduces it to extinction.

Two animals are characteristic of, and not uncommon on, the higher rocky slopes. The Himalayan Tahr which rather resembles a great shaggy goat occurs in herds or groups usually not far below the snowline, grazing particularly where the yaks have not reached. Although they are quite common, you have to look hard to see them. The Serow is another of the goat antelopes, like the Goral, and it is much smaller and less hairy than the Tahr, with short backward-sloping horns. This usually occurs singly or in pairs, at lower altitudes than the Tahr, sometimes in forested areas.

At the very highest altitudes, there are few other mammals which the exceptionally fortunate trekker may see. The Blue sheep haunts high ridges and valleys, and – though not uncommon in a few areas such as Shey in Dolpo – it is rarely seen. They occur in flocks, and may be quite tame where they are not hunted. A much larger animal is the Great Tibetan sheep, a race of the Argali (which includes the famous Marco Polo sheep of the Pamirs), though it is doubtful if this still occurs in Nepal. The rare and exceptionally beautiful Snow leopard still occurs all along the Himalayas, and although it is active in the day, it has only been photographed in the wild twice, which gives an indication of the chances of seeing it! Wolves are distinctly more common, and have been recorded up to 21,500 feet.

Perhaps the oddest of all the animal communities in the Himalayas is the small group of inter-dependent invertebrates that exists at 22,000 feet, well above the permanent snowline, under extreme weather conditions. Here, jumping spiders live on springtails and primitive flies, which in turn live on wind-blown detritus funnelled up from the lower slopes, and the whole community exists in equilibrium on ground which is snow-covered right through the year.

Two other animals should be mentioned before leaving this area, as both have contributed much to the fame of Nepal. The first is the yak. It is just possible that a few genuinely Wild yak still occur in trans-Himalayan areas of Nepal, such as Charkhabot, but all other yaks are domestic, even though some may resemble the genuine Wild yak. Pure yaks are of a uniform colour, dark brown to black, with unbelievably shaggy fur. They are crossed with cattle to produce a range of mottled hybrids bearing various names, such as Zopkio, Dzopo, Zo, giving animals with different combinations of hardiness, milk-bearing capacity and tractability. The yak and its hybrids are easily the most important animals of the high areas of Nepal for food, wool, and as beasts of burden.

Lastly, an animal of which no photographs at all exist, but which every visitor to Nepal still hopes to see – the Yeti, or Abominable Snowman! We do not have space to go into the detailed arguments that have taken place on whether or not the Yeti exists, and if so, what manner of animal it is. Expeditions have been mounted specifically to seek it out, and a great deal has been written about it, but no firm evidence of its existence has been found to date. Does it really exist then? With more and more people taking to the hills every year all over Nepal, the sceptic will ask why no visitor has definitely seen it. Two things are worth remembering here, though. Any mammal that has no recognizable lair, lives in wild country and times its activities to avoid man, can easily escape detection. How many people have seen a wild otter, in Britain for instance? And secondly, it is important to remember that new mammals are still being discovered in the world. Close at hand, and particularly relevant, is the discovery by E. P. Gee of the Golden Langur in Assam in 1955.

There are reports that an ape/man-like creature, unknown to science of course, exists in Tibet, and is occasionally seen at water-holes. Its existence is accepted without question by the local people. It is possible, therefore, that the infrequency of recorded sightings in Nepal is due to the fact that the population is based in Tibet, and animals only occasionally stray across the Himalayas by chance, or perhaps under adverse conditions. If they lived at high altitudes on the Nepalese side, there would surely have been more than the handful of reports of unidentified footprints in the snow from some of the numerous high altitude mountaineering expeditions.

The controversy will never be settled until the Yeti has been shown to exist, so keep those binoculars and telephotos handy while travelling in the high Himalayas. You never know.

Bird Life

The birdwatcher in Nepal, whether casual or serious, is the most fortunate of all visiting naturalists. Not only are there about 800 species of bird to be seen from tropical hornbills and peacocks to high altitude choughs and lammergeiers, but there is, since 1976, a detailed colour field guide to all the birds of Nepal. No other group of animals or plants in the country is covered in anything like the same detail, and most are not covered at all. The existence of this book makes a detailed description of the bird life superfluous, and impossible anyway, though it is worth mentioning a few of the more abundant species, to whet the traveller's appetite. Rather than picking a few species from the many over the whole country, we have instead concentrated on the Kathmandu birds and contrasted these with a typical high altitude bird-list.

The Kathmandu valley boasts a fortunate mixture of tropical, sub-tropical and temperate birds, which, when combined with the non-resident migrant species makes for exciting bird-watching. Over 400 species have been recorded from the valley area alone, and an annual Christmas Day bird count has now turned up nearly 200 bird species in Kathmandu in a single day! Hotel windows or flat roofs provide excellent viewing points for the fliers. Black kites, vultures, buzzards, eagles, and occasionally harriers soar overhead in the thermals, constantly watching for carrion; swallows, martins and swifts race about everywhere, and bright white egrets ply back and forth from their colonies to the rivers and wet fields. Cattle egrets with their orange-brown markings are common, too. Then a pair of spotted doves, with their characteristic speckled collars, may fly quickly across to settle in a tree. A loud burst of song heralds the presence of the jaunty little black and white Magpie robin. This aptly named bird is common around the city, and has a habit of starting to sing at about 4.30 or 5 a.m. outside the window. The Common mynah is a brown starling-like bird, with a yellowish eye patch, which is always in evidence, scavenging, screeching and jostling, and eating almost anything. Another abundant bird of city life is the House crow, black but with grey nape and breast, and very cheeky and tame. Smallish green birds, with a strange tuft of hairs at the base of their beak, are barbets of various species, found wherever there are woods or scattered trees.

A walk out to the edge of the houses, or along a river bank, is bound to turn up a few drongos, usually the Black drongo. They are elegant black birds, with a long forked tail, and a habit of perching on wires from where they chase insects. Along the river banks there are waders in plenty, varying according to season, but amongst which are many that are familiar to Europeans, such as Common and Green sandpipers, redshank and little stint. In more wooded areas, cuckoos of several species are common, particularly the Eurasian cuckoo ('Cuck-oo') and the Indian cuckoo (a melodic 'one more bot-tle'). Golden orioles warble, hidden in the depths of trees, while a small dark crested bird, with red below the tail, and a long chattering song, is the Red-vented bulbul.

In contrast, the birds of a high-altitude village such as Namche Bazaar, Tengboche, or Langtang are considerably more sparse, though full of interest. The all-black Jungle crow is common in villages, perching on roofs to watch for refuse and carrion. The much larger and shaggier raven is less common, and much less tame, preferring its own company to that of humans. Relatives of the crows and ravens are the choughs, and two very similar species occur at these heights, both in noisy flocks around cliffs and villages. These are the Red-billed chough and the Yellow-billed chough, and although both are black with red legs, they have different-coloured beaks and slightly different habits. The pale almost silver Snow pigeon occurs in large flocks in open fields around villages, leaving at night to roost on high ledges, often above the snowline, away from predators. Bearded vultures, or lammergeiers, are huge birds with a 9-foot wingspan, a diamond-shaped tail, and a golden head, and are often seen gliding gracefully along a hillside, or over the village refuse area. The Himalayan Griffon vulture is a much heavier, darker bird, almost rectangular in shape, which is quite common at high altitudes. Golden eagles may also be seen in the mountains, and have been recorded at great heights by climbing expeditions.

A characteristic bird of forests and forest edges, often near villages, and especially common between Namche Bazaar and Tengboche, is the extraordinary Danphe bird or Impeyan pheasant. If a heavy blue, green and orange bird, with a turquoise crest breaks cover with a noisy cackle, and glides off down the hillside, then this is a male of Nepal's national bird, the Danphe bird. Close relatives of it, though much less often seen, are the Snow partridge and the larger Tibetan snowcock, both of which can be seen well at and around Kala Pattar and Everest Base Camp.

Around the rivers, there are both Plumbeous and Blue-fronted redstarts, White-capped river chats and others, but a bird demanding attention whenever it is seen is the ibisbill. This is a very large, greyish wader, with a long red downward-curving beak, which nests on high altitude river shingle, in the flat glacial valleys. Besides all the commoner species, anything can occur. Many of the valleys are migration routes, and we have come across a Demoiselle crane at 14,000 feet near Everest, forced down by unusual weather, and new records are always possible for the alert observer.

Insect Life

At least a brief mention should be made of Nepal's incredible variety of insect life. Like almost everything else about Nepal, it is colourful and varied, and forces itself on your attention. Luckily, there are no real problems with biting insects in Nepal, except for mosquitoes in a few areas, but there is a bewildering variety of butterflies, brightly coloured beetles, damselflies and dragonflies and many others to be seen, while crickets and cicadas can usually be heard. Little is known about most of the groups of insects here, though the total number of different species must run into tens of thousands. There are for instance, over 500 species of butterfly, and it is only these that we shall mention further.

There are butterflies in Nepal from the Terai right up to, and past, the snowline, and as usual we can do no more than pick out a few highlights, and suggest ways to get to see them. Butterflies like warm weather, and many fly only when the sun is out, so it follows that the best times to see butterflies are April to June, September to October and during sunny periods in the monsoon, although they are about in warmer areas right through the winter. The variety in the sub-tropical areas are too great to get to know under normal circum-stances, though mention should be made of the great Golden birdwing. This rather uncommon butterfly has an eight to nine inch wingspan, and may be seen by the lucky visitor to Chitwan or elsewhere in the Terai.

In the Kathmandu area, the best place to see butterflies is at Godavari, especially around the beautiful botanic gardens there,

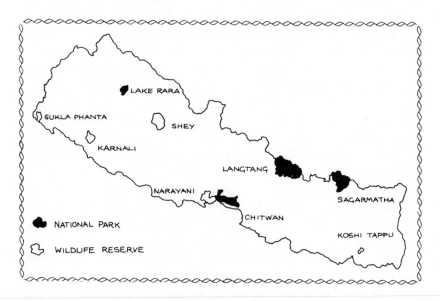

National parks and wildlife reserves in Nepal

and on the surrounding wooded hills to the southwest of the valley. There is a marvellous variety here, and many of them can be approached quite closely. The Long-tailed swallowtails, birdwings, clouded yellows, and many others can be seen and appreciated at their best here. It is also a fine area for flowers (as you might expect) and bird life, so it is well worth making the trip from Kathmandu, though it is out of normal walking range.

There are butterflies right up through the cultivated areas and mountain forests, and at and around the snowline there are the Apollos. These medium-sized black and white butterflies can be seen on the earliest spring flowers where the snow has melted, and are quite often seen flying over the snow up to 18,000 feet. A good place for these is at the sacred lakes of Gosainkund, at 14,000 feet in the mountains to the north of Kathmandu, where we spent a marvellous sunny day in April watching apollos, tortoiseshells, and the first bees on the flowers of the early gentians and primulas just below the snow.

National Parks and Wildlife Conservation

It is something of a truism that conservation is the prerogative of the rich, so, since Nepal is listed by the United Nations as one of the twenty-five poorest countries in the world, it is not surprising that conservation of resources for their own sake has not been high on the Nepalese list of priorities until recently. But, over the last ten or fifteen years, an ambitious programme of conservation has been embarked upon by the far-sighted Nepalese government, in conjunction with the United Nations, the World Wildlife Fund, the New Zealand government and many other national and international groups. The main aim has been to survey those areas most in need of protection, and to establish a selection of protected regions as representatives of the different habitat types occurring in the country. At present, there are four national parks and five wildlife reserves established in Nepal, with a total area of almost 1700 square miles. The problems of making these into practical protected units in a country with considerable geographical and climatic extremes, and a population unused to the discipline that such areas demand, can perhaps be imagined, but solutions are gradually being discovered both by trial and error, and by learning from other countries. It is becoming apparent in Chitwan and Sagarmatha just what can be done, and detailed and far-reaching proposals for Langtang have recently been completed.

But the casual visitor might well enquire why all this effort should be necessary for a country like Nepal. There is, by most standards, hardly any heavy industry or roads, there is teeming bird and plant life, large areas of virgin forest, flower-strewn mountain pastures, and a general air of peaceful equilibrium. It is easy to think of the Nepalese as a long-established people living in close harmony with nature, with little change taking place over thousands of years. But, sadly, this is far from being the case. A gradual reduction in the acreage of unspoilt areas will have been taking place for centuries, but in the last few decades there have been several dramatic changes which have vastly broadened this deterioration.

Once, the Terai was the greatest hunting-ground in Asia, particularly in the Rapti and Narayani valleys. Huge bags of game, including numerous specimens of the tiger and the extremely scarce Indian One-horned rhinoceros, were recorded during the first half of this century. The area was kept as a preserve of the Ranas, the hereditary prime ministers, so that, although accorded considerable protection in many ways, the numbers of animals killed every so often were very high. Visiting European royalty and nobility, expecially British ones, were entertained at huge hunting parties, before conservation became fashionable, and these brought about the greatest slaughter. However, the general infrequency of the hunting, and the overall protection of the areas ensured that good stocks of game remained and that the vegetation was undisturbed. Until quite recently, too, the Terai was infested with malaria, and inhabited only by the partially resistant Tharu peoples. But by 1959, over 12,000 farmers had been officially recorded as settling in land that was previously virgin forest, and no doubt many more went unrecorded. They came down from the hills, where cultivation is a constant struggle against the slopes and the elements, to take advantage of the flat fertile land that had become accessible. It is surprising, though, how long the fear of malaria has persisted. Even quite recently, it was not uncommon to hear first-hand accounts of hill people who, although ill or dying, would refuse to go down to the lowlands for treatment, because they feared the dreaded malaria, long since eradicated, more than anything.

The overthrow of the Ranas, and the opening of the country to tourists since the 1950s brought about many far-reaching changes. For wildlife and plants, the tourists are a mixed blessing. It is true that tourists bring much-needed funds, allowing the government time and money to give thought to conservation. In addition, as in

Africa, tourism is one of the pressures behind the formation of national parks and other conserved areas because they quickly become major tourist attractions. But, on the other hand, the changes that tourism brings are many and varied, pervading all aspects of the country, unless considerable care is taken to prevent it. Most insidious perhaps is the changes it brings about in the lifestyle and outlook of the people it comes into contact with. Traditional farming and home industry may be discarded for the quicker gains of the tourist-associated industries; religious ideas on the sanctity of life may be forgotten in the pursuit of easy money, and everything may be sacrificed to the great god of tourism and its dollars. This is happening to some extent in Nepal, though it is by no means as bad as it might be, yet it is difficult to know what the individual visitor can do about it. It is mostly a matter for governmental policy, international aid, and the nature of the people themselves.

It is unwise to think of conservation as a luxury, or as a mere waste of time and money on preserving a few useless animals doomed to extinction anyway. Views on the conservation of rare mammals differ considerably, though we believe strongly that no species should knowingly be allowed to become extinct. Here, however, we are concerned with the conservation of a whole environment, and the far-reaching effects that changes in a balanced environment can bring. We cannot go into details of the whole complex of changes that take place, but it is worth considering the way in which one aspect of Nepalese life can affect everything else.

The Nepalese have always used trees as firewood, as building material, and to some extent as fodder. But the increase in population, and the considerable increase in visiting tourists has brought about a vastly increased demand, which is not met by existing traditional supplies. The forests around villages are the first to go, and many villagers now have to travel miles for their wood, where once it was on the edge of the village. The price of wood in the hills has rocketed in the past few years, but the overall effects of the shortage are much more important. Forests act as natural sponges, or buffers, and they soak up heavy rainfall, preventing it from running straight off the steep hillsides, and releasing it gently all through the year. So, wherever there are large cleared treeless areas, there are now regular landslips during the monsoon, and the village water supplies may dry up during the winter, where once they ran all the year round. All the soil that is washed from the denuded hillsides, whether in landslips or trickles, has to go somewhere, and it ends up in the streams and rivers. It is swept along, through the fast-flowing stretches in the hills, and is deposited later as the waters slow down on reaching the flat plains. As a consequence, dams silt up, and river courses become even wider and more complex. Because the normal pattern of seasonal run-off is being altered all along the mountains, and relatively few main rivers drain the area, the combined effects can be considerable. There are already more serious floods in the Terai than ever before, and the situation will only get worse if clearance proceeds. In addition, natural regeneration cannot take place, as more animals are being grazed on and around the cleared areas, preventing the seedling trees from getting started.

There are solutions, but they involve complex social, ecological and organizational issues, and will be some years before the many trials taking place bear fruit. We hope that anyone visiting Nepal will at least give thought to ways in which they can help to prevent the situation worsening. Nepal is one of the most beautiful countries in the world, and much of it remains completely unspoilt still. It would be a tragedy if too many thoughtless visitors changed all that. To the hill villager, it is simply a nuisance, a whim of the gods, that he has to travel further, and spend more of his day in getting his wood. But that is only where the problem starts.

Sagarmatha National Park
This is Nepal's mountain showpiece. Almost 500 square miles of the highest area in the world, and including the highest mountain in the world, were declared as Nepal's second national park. It contains a complex of high mountains, glaciers and valleys extending south from Mount Everest (the Sherpa name for which is Sagarmatha), and containing most of the headwaters of the Dudh Kosi. In addition to the obvious attractions of mountains like Everest, Cho Dyo, Nuptse, Lhotse and Amu Dablang, the area is also the homeland of the famous Sherpas, and is notable for the presence of some of the best-known and most attractive Buddhist monasteries in the world. When you add to this a rich variety of high-level forest with magnolias and rhododendrons, an abundance of bird and animal life, and spectacular scenery all around, it becomes obvious why it is considered to be one of the world's foremost national parks.

It was set up with considerble assistance from New Zealand, largely through Sir Edmund Hillary's close connections with the area, and there is now an ambitious programme of conservation and education measures taking place. Although there is a luxury high-altitude hotel in the area (Everest View run by Japanese and Nepalese), and two airstrips serve the park, it is unlikely that roads will ever be allowed to penetrate the higher reaches of the park. Access is by foot, usually from the 'Chinese road' to Lhasa, at Lamosangu, or by air to either Lukla or Sengboche STOL airstrips. The latter lies at over 12,000 feet, and great care should be taken to acclimatize gently if walking from here, as the dangers of altitude sickness are very real and considerable above these heights. There is now a permanently manned high altitude medical post at Pheriche, run by dedicated doctors and helpers, but no undue risks should be taken.

Langtang National Park
The Langtang area was officially declared as a national park in 1976, as Nepal's second mountain national park. It covers an area of over 500 square miles lying roughly north of Kathmandu, and running up to the Tibetan border. It is a spectacularly beautiful mountain area, containing the beautiful twin snow peaks of Langtang (23,770 feet and 21,592 feet) and the striking summit of Dorje Lhapka (22,929 feet), and the sacred lakes of Gosainkund lying at 14,000 feet around the headwaters of the Trisuli river.

The park area is a microcosm of Nepal, with a vast range of life from sub-tropical in the southwestern corner, above Betrawati, to high alpine and beyond, and containing people of many races including Thamang, Sherpa, and Bhotia. Apart from the trek up the Langtang valley, and that to Gosainkund and part of Helambu, the area is still largely unknown and unvisited.

Access is normally on foot, up the Trisuli and Langtang valleys from the end of the road at Trisuli or Betrawati, or by the more difficult route from the Helambu area. There is an airstrip at Kyangin, near the head of the Langtang valley, serving the cheese factory there, and helicopters often bring tourists to here and Ghoratabele. As the organization of the park gets under way, other facilities will be made available, though at present there are sufficient lodges to allow the visitor an easy trip stopping at a lodge every night, on the main trail.

Lake Rara National Park
The Lake Rara National Park is a national park with a difference. Although there are great plans for its future, it has, hitherto, been visited by very few people. Centred around the beautiful deep blue

Rara lake (Mah Tal), the park lies in a remote area of northwest Nepal to which access is often difficult and always unpredictable, and this, combined with the general ignorance of the possibilities of anything west of Pokhara, have ensured that the area has remained quiet and unspoilt.

The park comprises 40 square miles of forested hills around and to the south of the 4-square mile lake, Nepal's largest and deepest. Its particular importance is as a means of preserving this lake, but it is also the only preserved area where a good sample of the very different western forest type predominates. As previously explained, the west of Nepal is considerably drier than the east, and although Rara lies to the south of the main Himalayan chain, it is protected by range after range of lower hills, and the rainfall there is obviously considerably lower there than in the Langtang National Park for instance. The lake itself lies at 9800 feet, and much of the park lies at about this height, with no great peaks or valleys. The commonest tree around the lake is the Blue pine (*Pinus excelsa*), often mixed in with other conifers such as spruce, fir, and juniper higher up, and giving way to deciduous oaks, walnuts and horse chestnuts on the valley bottoms. The general appearance is much less lush than equivalent forests in eastern Nepal, and the number of flowers is considerably lower here.

The wildlife is not exceptionally rich, being similar to, though poorer than that of the Langtang park. The alert visitor may see, with a bit of luck, jackals, Wild dogs, Black bears, Musk deer, goral or serow. More likely, one will see little except a few droppings or tracks. Langur monkeys are there, of course, and rarer denizens include the Red panda and the leopard. Bird life is quite rich, as one would expect at this height in Nepal, and things to look out for in particular here include the Tibetan snowcock, and a reasonable number of resident and migrant waterbirds such as Bar-Headed geese, Ruddy shelduck (both on their way to and from Tibet), and grebes.

The Park is well worth a visit for its solitude, and remoteness, if nothing else, and anything of interest recorded should be passed on to the National Parks Department – it could easily be a new record.

Chitwan National Park
The Royal Chitwan National Park was Nepal's first national park, and it is undoubtedly the richest area in the country for wildlife. At present, it covers an area of 210 square miles, more or less on the site

of an old royal hunting reserve, though a large westward extension of the park is now under preparation. The outstanding features of its wildlife have already been described.

The park is easily accessible by air from Kathmandu, or by road, and there are now a variety of places to stay or camp, in addition to the original tigertops, such as the Gaida Wildlife Camp (*Gaida* is the Nepalese name for the One-horned rhinoceros that occurs in the park). From the climatic point of view, it is best to visit Chitwan between October and March, when it is not too hot. Viewed either as an area filled with an incredible variety of wildlife, birds, plants and insects, or as a historical relict of what the whole upper Ganges must once have been like, Chitwan is an extraordinary place, and a definite 'must' on many tourist itineraries.

Wildlife Reserves

Five wildlife reserves have now been proposed or declared in Nepal, covering an area of about 475 square miles. Each one contains some particular rare species, or group of species, thought they are considerably smaller than the national parks.

Sukla Phanta Wildlife Reserve

The Sukla Phanta reserve is a roughly circular area of about 60 square miles in the extreme western Terai, around the Muhakeli river. Besides containing a good sample of typical Terai vegetation, it is of particular value for the protection it gives to one of the last remaining herds of Swamp deer (Barasingha) in Asia and the only one in Nepal. It is an attractive area of grassland and forest, and it is also a good place to see tiger, leopard, sambar, chital, nilgai, Hog-deer, and such rare birds as the Swamp partridge.

Karnali Wildlife Reserve

The 140 or so square miles of this reserve lie on the site of an old hunting reserve, which is both an indication of its richness and a measure of the protection it has been given in the past. It lies on the east bank of the Karnali river in western Nepal, and contains the largest remaining population of tigers left in Nepal. There are also good-sized areas of sal forest, and an abundance of the usual Terai mammals, such as chital, sambar, nilgai, leopard and bear.

Koshi Tappu Wildlife Reserve

This is the smallest of the proposed wildlife reserves, at about 12 square miles. It is an area of seasonally flooded grassland and scattered trees on the banks of the Kosi river in east Nepal, and it was set up particularly to protect the herd of forty or so last remaining Water buffalo in Nepal. Although small in area, there is also a good variety of other Terai mammals, birds and plants.

Shey Wildlife Reserve
This reserve consists of 160 square miles of wild country in the trans-Himalayan Dolpo district of western Nepal, at 12,000 to 18,000 feet. It is being preserved as a sample of the dry trans-Himalayan ecosystem, and is notable for the presence of large numbers of Himalayan marmots, Blue sheep, Tibetan snowcock, and similar high altitude species. It is unlikely that access to the reserve will be possible in the near future.

Narayani Wildlife Reserve
This is an area, of about 100 square miles, that has been added to the Chitwan National Park to provide additional protection for tigers, rhinos and other Terai species.

6. Bhutan: Background Notes

Bhutan covers an area of about 18,000 square miles, comparable to the area of Switzerland, and it supports a population of just over one million people. It is, perhaps, the closest approach to the Himalayan shangri-la, for it has remained more closed, and for longer, than any of its neighbours, yet it harbours an atmosphere of peace and friendship in its villages and monasetries, set amongst some of the most impressive scenery in the world. Even the British in India found it difficult to enter, more so than neighbouring Tibet, and it is only in the last few years, since 1974, that foreign tourists have been allowed to enter the country in any significant numbers.

Bhutan's policy in joining the modern world has been to take everything in moderation, learning from the mistakes of others, and this same policy has applied to the opportunity presented by tourism – Bhutan is feeling its way, balancing the advantages against the problems, and many parts of this extraordinary country are still closed to the visitor. Nevertheless, for the lucky few a visit to Bhutan is one of the most unusual experiences that the world has to offer.

Like Nepal, Bhutan lies along the Himalayan chain, and it encompasses within its boundaries the whole range of altitudes from a few hundred feet to over 24,000 feet. It can be clearly divided into three regions.

The Duars plain, comparable with the Terai of Nepal, and contiguous with the Indian plains, is a strip some eight to ten miles wide along Bhutan's southern border with India. This area has always had a very low population, because of the problems of disease, especially malaria, and the more attractive land still available elsewhere. But as the population has increased, malaria has been conquered, and settlers with a knowledge of farming in such areas have come in, so this area has begun to be settled and cleared, and towns like Phuntsholing have begun to spread. Much remains virgin, however, and areas like the Manas Game Reserve (62 square miles) have been set aside to preserve them.

The rainfall here is high, especially where the hills rise out of the plain, though as usual it is very seasonal with most of the rain coming in the summer. Most villages are clustered around the base of the hills, where crops of rice and tropical fruits are grown.

The central area of Bhutan is generally called the inner Himalayas, and it is here that the main centres of Bhutan (such as they are) are found. It is broadly comparable with the midlands of Nepal, but generally at a higher altitude. The area consists essentially of a series of spurs radiating south from the Great Himalayas, including for example the Black Mountains between the Sankosh and Manas rivers, together with the fertile valleys between them. The southernmost ramparts rise dramatically and steeply from the Duars plain. There is remarkably little flat land, and virtually all farming and settlement is confined to the broad alluvial valleys. Unlike Nepal, there are not terraces up every slope, because the population density has always been lower. The area is enormously diverse, not only because of the great altitude range and variety of aspects, but also because of the variation in rainfall. Parts of the region are in the rainshadow of the southernmost ranges, and the rainfall is only 40 to 50 inches per annum, while some of the higher and more exposed ridges receive up to 150 inches. There is, consequently, a great variation in the vegetation. The inner Himalayan area is the most populous part of Bhutan, and it is here that the capital Thimpu lies, in a broad fertile valley at about 7600 feet.

Other main towns in the inner Himalayas include Bumthang and Tashigang. The basis of life in these middle hills is agriculture, with a variety of crops such as rice, buckwheat, maize and wheat being grown, with increasing numbers of fruit orchards, and now limited industrial production.

North of the inner Himalayas lies the Great Himalayas, a region of high peaks and glaciers reaching up to the Chinese (Tibetan) border. Much of the land is over 18,000 feet, and several peaks reach 24,000 feet. There is also a small area of trans-Himalayan plateau, though much less than in Nepal. Not surprisingly, few people live here. Once there was a flourishing trade with Tibet in yaks, salt, wool and other products, but this has ceased since the Chinese occupation. There are still subsistence yak herders in the area (and it is rumoured that some herders even farm the wild Blue sheep that

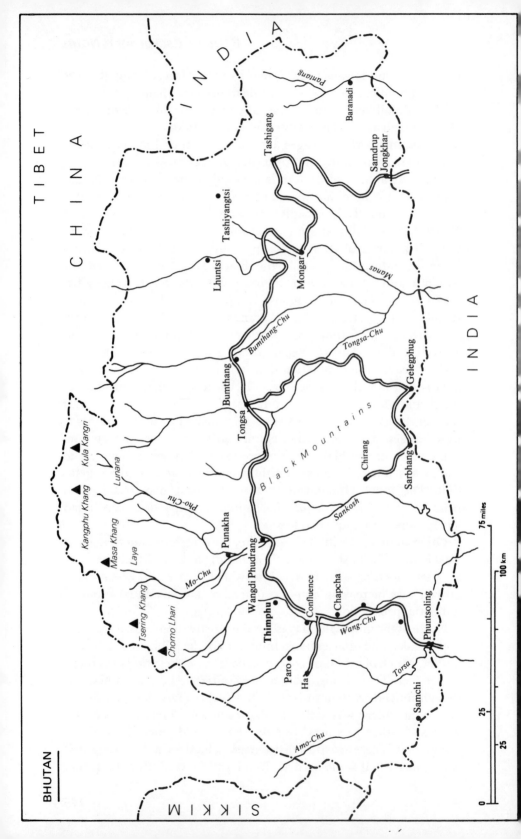

abound in parts), together with a few recent Tibetan refugee settlements, and some military outposts.

It is a remarkably undisturbed area, with few signs of man, and with persistent reports of isolated so-called Stone-Age tribes living along the northern and eastern borders. It is, without doubt, one of the remotest and least-visited parts of the terrestrial world. Most peaks are unclimbed and unvisited, and some are not even named. The main peaks are Chomolhari (24,000 feet) close to the Chumbi valley of Tibet, Kangphu Kang (23,800 feet), and Kula Kangri (24,800 feet). The latter two lie in the central high altitude area known as Lunana, a strangely apt name for a desolate and uninhabited area of high peaks, glaciers and glacial lakes.

It must be clear from this description of the terrain of Bhutan that, with the exception of the narrow Duars strip along the southern border, the country has a remarkable circle of natural barriers which have closed it off from the rest of the world, and which have helped Bhutan to retain its identity, even when disunion reigned within the country.

The climate of Bhutan differs little from that of Nepal (see Chapter 2). It is a monsoon-dominated climate, with the same summer wet season and dry autumn and winter, and with the same gradual build-up of dust, heat and thunderstorms through spring towards the onset of the monsoon in June. The main differences from Nepal lie in Bhutan's more easterly position, and greater proximity to the sea at the Bay of Bengal. It also has less protective land mass and fewer outlying hills than Nepal, so the net result is that it is wetter overall than Nepal, though a few of the inner valleys are remarkably dry.

Thus, the same advice for the intending visitor applies: October–November for good weather and fabulous clear views; winter is clear and cold, more noticeably so than in Nepal because the main centres are at higher altitudes; spring is another good time to go, with rhododendrons and other flowers everywhere, but increasing haze and thundery rain as the monsoon approaches. The summer, finally, is the monsoon period and Bhutan suffers from all the same problems as east and central Nepal.

Compared to Nepal, the ethnic diversity of Bhutan is limited, though the origins of some of the races are equally obscure. There are three broad ethnic groups in Bhutan, though the distinctions blur in places. The Sharchops are believed to be the earliest inhabitants of the country; they are of Indo-Mongolian type, though their exact origins are uncertain, with Tibet as the most likely source. At present they live mainly in the east of Bhutan. The Ngalops are the descendants of more recent immigrants from Tibet, who entered Bhutan at various periods from the ninth century onwards and settled there, bringing their customs and religion with them. They now live mainly in the west and centre of the country. These two groups, the Sharchops and the Ngalops, are sometimes collectively known as the Bhutias or Bhotes, and they account for over half of the population.

The third group is the Nepalese, living mainly in the south and west of the country, having settled there from the end of the nineteenth century onwards. The settlers were mainly from the Rai, Limbu or Gurung tribes of Nepalese, from the east and centre of the country. They brought the Hindu religion with them, and the Nepalese language, which is still spoken today over much of the southern part of Bhutan. There is not the same mingling of Hindu and Buddhist religions that we can see in Nepal, and the two tend to keep apart. Indeed, settlers of Nepalese origin, even if Bhutanese citizens, are prohibited from settling in central Bhutan, and all Nepalese immigration has been stopped since 1959. Not surprisingly, this has led to some friction and dissent amongst the Nepalese-origin Bhutanese citizens, who feel discriminated against, though it is an indication of Bhutan's strong desire to retain its national identity.

Bhutan's official language is Dzongkha, essentially a dialect of Tibetan, and it is written in classical Ucan Tibetan script, though it has acquired numerous minor differences from Tibetan over the centuries. English is the language of instruction in many schools, so it is widely spoken in central Bhutan, while Nepali is spoken in the south. A classical form of Dzongkha, Cheokay, is used in monastic schools. Because of the isolation of valleys within Bhutan from each other, a number of dialects, frequently mutually unintelligible, have arisen, especially in the east, and this has hindered the unification of the country, though new roads and a more available system of education are tending to break down these differences now. It is estimated that in eastern Bhutan there are eleven different dialects, though the language of Bhutan has not been closely studied, and some may well prove to be different languages rather than simply dialects. It is certain, however, that there is much less variation than in Nepal.

One of the special features of the country, and one which is almost unique to Bhutan, is the presence throughout the country of numerous dzongs. Dzongs are hybrids between monasteries and forts – not dissimilar to the potala in Lhasa – varying between the strongly fortified and the more monastic type. They are all different, yet they are all based loosely on the pattern of the first one, the Simtokha Dzong, at the entrance to the Thimpu valley, which was built by Ngawang Namgyal in 1627. Shortly after the first one was built, numerous others were built around the country, and they have continued to be added to, repaired, and even built, right up to the present day, culminating in the construction of the enormous Tashichhodzong in Thimpu in 1970, to house the government offices.

Intriguingly, the classical method of construction involves no nails, and no plans are drawn to assist in their design. The pattern varies according to ground conditions, but most share the imposing looks, the tapering walls, and the multiplicity of temples, galleries and courtyards within. Some clearly served a strategic function when they were constructed, serving as a retreat for the local population in times of difficulty, while others have the appearance of classical monasteries. The dzongs themselves were normally built in the valleys, often at a confluence of rivers, and built above them were small round fortress watchtowers known as Ta Dzongs. One of these, above the Paro Dzong, is now the national musuem of Bhutan. Perhaps the most spectacular of the dzongs is the Tongsa Dzong, which tumbles down a hillside above the Tongsa river in a series of storeys. It was originally built in 1648, though it has been constantly added to, and today it contains twenty separate temples.

Elsewhere, there are more simple temples or monasteries scattered throughout the country, often located in the most extraordinary of places. One of the most famous, and perhaps the most spectacularly located, is the Taktsang monastery, or 'Tiger's Nest', perched on a ledge near the top of a sheer 3000 foot cliff, accessible only by a steep narrow path (see Chapter 9).

Lastly amongst Bhutan's numerous attractions for the visitor its natural history must be mentioned. The general pattern of the vegetation and natural history of the region has been described for Nepal (see Chapter 5). Bhutan's natural life is similar, though even more varied and even less well known. Bhutan is richer for two main reasons: firstly, it lies further east along the Himalayan chain, and there is a general trend for the number of species to increase as the rainfall increases eastwards; and secondly there is a much greater proportion of the natural vegetation remaining in Bhutan than Nepal, reflecting the lower population density and less intensive cultivation. There are less of the cosmopolitan species, and less of the species dependent on dwellings and agriculture, and many of the drought-tolerant species of west and north Nepal are absent, but in other respects the natural history of Bhutan is richer. There are, for example, many more species of primula and rhododendron, and a much greater variety of orchids, with a profusion of other species of plant from sub-tropical to high alpine types. Birds are less well recorded than in Nepal, though we have found that we recorded more species in a given period in Bhutan than Nepal (Fleming's excellent book on the birds of Nepal covers many of the species found in Bhutan), and it is generally easier to see species because they are tamer and more abundant. Choughs (both species) are abundant everywhere, for example, and impressive species like Himalayan nutcrackers are readily visible in most patches of middle altitude forest, including from the rooms of some of the hotels! Larger raptors and vultures are common, and lammergeiers, eagles and so on are a common sight. There is a wide range of pheasants, and most days in the mountains and forests will reveal a few species, notably Kalij and Blood pheasants.

Mammals too are more in evidence than in Nepal. Deer are widespread and abundant, notably Barking deer, but also Musk deer and others. It is a common sight to see Barking deer crossing roads or trails, and even in the grounds of some of the hotels. Blue sheep, which are so rare in most of Nepal, are common in some areas, and trekkers to Chomolhari Base Camp often come across herds of a hundred or so animals, a beautiful sight. Snow leopards occur at the highest altitudes, and various Big Cats from jungle cat to leopard are often seen in the middle altitude forests. Bears, too, are more frequently seen than in Nepal.

Lower down, the wildlife is equally varied. The Duars area of Bhutan has most of the species of Nepal, and a few more besides, including a few that are endemic to the area. The Manas sanctuary, for example, has populations of tiger, crocodiles, Pigmy hog, wild elephant, leopard, and the rare and only recently discovered Golden langur, confined to Bhutan and adjacent Assam. Again, species tend to be more abundant than in Nepal (e.g. in Chitwan) because they are less disturbed and there is less competition from domestic grazing animals.

All in all, Bhutan is a remarkable place, a strange survival from medieval times with much of the character of the fabled shangri-la feeling its way gently into a union with the rest of the world.

7. Bhutan's History and Religion

In Bhutan, as in Nepal and Sikkim, religion and history are closely intertwined. Sadly, the history of Bhutan is not as well documented now as it once was, for most of the irreplaceable Namthar (ancient printing blocks) of the national archive were destroyed in fires in Sonagatsel in 1828 and Punakha in 1832. This was followed by the destruction of many of those remaining by a major earthquake in 1896 and another fire in Paro Dzong a few years later. Almost the whole of this remarkable record of the history of Bhutan under Buddhism and even before had been destroyed. So, our knowledge of the history of Bhutan depends on the remaining Namthar, a few artefacts, the histories of adjacent countries, and some conjecture.

There is archaeological evidence of very early civilizations within the boundaries of present-day Bhutan, but we discover any detailed records for the first time in AD 450–600. At this time, the religion of Bonism was introduced into Bhutan from Tibet – Bonism was the original religion of Tibet, before the introduction of Buddhism, and it involved a form of spirit worship coupled with magic practices. Typically of religions in this area, many of its rituals became absorbed into later religions, despite their totally different basis, and some features of the old Bon religion persist to modern times in parts of the country (and elsewhere in the Himalayas). The animist religions of Bon and related religions were dominant until the introduction of Buddhism to Bhutan in the eighth century, and it is this religion that has dominated the spiritual and cultural path that Bhutan has followed ever since.

Bhutan's 'historical' period begins at about AD 747 when the revered religious leader Guru Padma Sambhava came from Tibet and introduced Buddhism to the country. Known also to the Bhutanese as Guru Rimpoche, this remarkable man who is almost as highly esteemed as Buddha himself in Bhutan, is credited with various events. It is said, for example, that he flew to Bhutan on the back of a tiger, and that at Taktsang he conquered the demon spirits that were standing in the way of the spread of Buddhism. For this reason, the monastery at Taktsang, clinging dizzily to a 3000 foot cliff-face, is known as the Tiger's Nest. It is more certain, however, that he visited Bumthang in central Bhutan (where he cured the ailing king), and various places in the Paro valley, and that he and his later followers meditated in a cave on the cliff where Taktsang monastery now stands. In Bumthang, the Kurje temple was built at the spot where, after Padma Sambhava had meditated, his finger-prints and footmarks appeared etched into solid rock, and where a cypress tree (which still stands) sprouted from his staff.

At all events, it is clear that Guru Padma Sambhava had an enormous influence on religion in Bhutan, and he is still worshipped today. His teachings were so precious that they were known as *Termas*, or treasures, to be hidden and safeguarded in difficult times. It is for this reason that Bhutan came to be known as 'Land of Hidden Treasures', a name often misinterpreted by the avaricious.

The pattern of Buddhism has changed considerably over the centuries, influenced particularly by emigrants from Tibet at first, later developing its own forms. Padma Sambhava introduced Buddhism of the Nyingmapa sect – the old sect – but changes and divisions in the religion in Tibet were so fierce that this was quickly influenced by other sects, driven out first by non-Buddhist rulers like Langdarma (king of Tibet in the ninth century) then later by rival Buddhist sects.

By the eleventh century, Buddhism was universally established in Tibet, and three distinct schools had arisen: the original Nyingmapa school; the Kahdampa (which, renamed as the Gelugpa school, would ultimately become the dominant form in Tibet, with the Dalai Lama at its head); and the Kagyupa school. Kagyupa practice was somewhat ascetic and rigorous, demanding long periods of isolation and meditation such that various less demanding sub-sects arose. Amongst these was the Drukpa ('Thunder Dragon') sub-sect, so named it is said because thunder echoed across the sky when it was being formed. It is this sect – the Drukpa sect of Kagyupa, a branch of Mahayana ('Greater Vehicle') Buddhism, to give it its full title – that has since become the dominant religion in Bhutan, and which is now the official religion.

However, back in the twelfth century and succeeding ones, waves of Lamas from the Drukpa Kagyupa or the Lhapa Kagyupa continued to come from Tibet, either as missionaries, or fleeing from persecution by the increasingly dominant Gelugpas (the 'Yellow Hats'). For a long time after this, the Drukpas and Lhapas shared the religious loyalties of the people, and there was a constant jostling and vying for power for one or the other.

During the whole of the period from the first introduction of Buddhism into Bhutan, and possibly well before, it seems likely that Bhutan existed as an independent entity, within similar natural boundaries to those that exist now. There was no central authority, however, and a number of separate towns or principalities existed, often practising different religions or different forms of the same religion, and with mutually unintelligible dialects or languages. Given the extraordinary physical barriers existing within the country, and the great difficulties of access and communication, it is hardly surprising that such a state of disunion should have existed. It is perhaps more surprising that a country of this nature should have become united so early in its history, and that it did so is due almost entirely to the efforts of one particularly forceful and far-sighted man, Ngawang Namgyal.

By 1600 or thereabouts, Gelugpa power in Tibet had extended as far as the Ralung monastery near Lhasa, religious centre of the Drukpa sect. The Drukpa Lamas were forced to flee or submit, and many of them found their way to Bhutan. Amongst these refugee Lamas was Ngawang Namgyal, who was to have a remarkable effect on his adopted land. He arrived in Bhutan in 1616, and at that time there was no central authority, no laws and no dominant religion, yet by the time he died in 1651, the whole of western Bhutan was under one government and five years later the whole country had one government and one religion – Drukpa Buddhism.

When he first arrived, Namgyal depended heavily for support on the many rich families in western Bhutan who already supported the Drukpas. As soon as he was assured of this support, he set about building a chain of dzongs (fortress monasteries) in all the main valleys of western Bhutan, starting with the Simtokha Dzong in the Thimpu valley. These rapidly became the focal points for civil and religious authority for each region, and remain one of the great features of the landscape and life of Bhutan today. In 1639, the king of Tsang in Tibet invaded Bhutan from the north, though Namgyal succeeded in uniting the Bhutanese sufficiently to rout the Tibetans in a great victory. After this victory, he assumed the title of Shabdung, the first, and he had effectively become the temporal and spiritual ruler of Bhutan.

His power was soon to be tested again. In 1644, the Mongol leader, Gushi Khan (who had, in 1642, defeated the king of Tsang and installed the Dalai Lama as spiritual leader of all Tibet) invaded Bhutan from the north with a vast army. Somehow he was repulsed, though he invaded again in 1647, and was again defeated. Not surprisingly, these successes served to strengthen the Shabdung's position, and to unite the country further. After establishing himself as Shabdung, Namgyal set about establishing a system of government and laws for the country. A Jey Khempo (head abbot) was appointed to manage the religious institutions, while civil power was invested in a Druk Desi, or Deb – a sort of prime minister. The country was divided into regions which were administered by governors known as Penlops (though initially called Philas), with Dzongpons appointed below them to administer civil affairs locally. At the same time, he drew up a comprehensive system of laws for the first time in the country.

Although he died in 1651, it is believed that the death of the Shabdung was officially kept a secret for over fifty years, in the hope that a legitimate successor might eventually be found. For the first few years, this presented no problems, and the unification of the country continued. But gradually power devolved onto the office of the Druk Desi, and wrangling and local civil wars ensued. The problem lay in the method of choosing successive Shabdungs; this lay in reincarnation, with all the difficulties that that presented in terms of recognizing the successor. At the same time the process contained the seeds of instability in that a successor was chosen at birth, so that for the first eighteen years of his rule he was a minor, and power again devolved onto the Druk Desi. Successive Druk Desis proved reluctant to part with the power when the Shabdung finally came of age, and the power of the Shabdung gradually waned. Namgyal's efforts at establishing a central authority were gradually wasted, as the Druk Desi lost control to the regional governors, the Penlops, and the country degenerated into a series of semi-independent regions, each controlled by a governor. The overall identity of Bhutan remained though, and the country could become united again when events demanded.

By the mid-eighteenth century, the power of the Moghuls in northern India was declining, and Bhutanese influence in the adjacent region of Cooch Behar increased, until by 1772 they held almost total control over the region. At this stage, they experienced their first contact with the British in India, a relationship which was to dominate their foreign affairs for nearly 200 years until the British withdrew. The British East India Company were anxious at this time to secure the northern frontiers of their domain, and they looked on the Bhutanese activities with disfavour. In 1773, a small British force was despatched to the area, with the connivance and financial backing of a pretender to the throne of Cooch Behar, Khagenda Narayan. This force, with its superior weapons and organization defeated the Bhutanese and forced them to withdraw. They also went one stage further and captured two Bhutanese forts in the foothills. Not surprisingly, this alarmed the Bhutanese, who hastily called on the Panchen Lama of Tibet to intercede with Warren Hastings, the governor-general of India at the time. This he agreed to do, and the negotiations led to the signing of a peace treaty between Bhutan and Britain, and a period of increased contact between the two countries. A series of missions were sent to Bhutan over a period of years, but then contact lapsed again.

Meanwhile, the Bhutanese desire for expansion turned elsewhere, particularly to the east. In Assam, still independent of the British at that time, the Ahom dynasty was in disarray and Bhutan found no difficulty in increasing its influence there. By 1826, the Bhutanese had gained control of all the passes (Duars) into Assam. In 1828, though, the British occupied Assam, and once more they came into contact with the Bhutanese. For years, there were minor clashes as the British gradually regained control of the Duars, and eventually this turned into the second Anglo-Bhutanese war. By 1865, however, the British were in control of all the passes in Bengal and Assam, and were in a position to push the Bhutanese back on all fronts. The war ended in 1865 with the Treaty of Sinchaula, which signalled the end of hostilities between the two countries, and provided for conditions of mutual peace and friendship. Trade became open and duty-free, Bhutan ceded all claims to the eighteen Duars, and received an annual payment of 50,000 rupees from the British government. This agreement has continued with independent India since the signing of a treaty in 1949.

As we have already mentioned, the power of the supreme authority, the Shabdung, and the civil leader, the Druk Desi (or Deb) had been gradually declining since Ngawang Namgyal had established the system in the seventeenth century. In the latter half of the nineteenth century, chaos more or less reigned, and the main power factions became centred on the governors (Penlops) of Paro and Tongsa, who had become the two most powerful men in the country. These two factions battled for power, with considerable disagreement between them on whether to maintain their traditional ties with Tibet, or whether to turn more to the British in India, with the Penlop of Paro favouring ties with Tibet. The British, inadvertently, helped to end the conflict and establish the hereditary monarchy that rules Bhutan today. In 1903, the Younghusband expedition was despatched to Lhasa, to make contact and open up trade with Tibet. On their way, they passed through Bhutan, and while the Penlop of Paro remained aloof, the current Penlop of Tongsa, Ugyen Wangchuck, welcomed them and offered every assistance. Ugyen Wangchuck also accompanied the expedition as far as Lhasa, and – through his contacts there – helped to negotiate a favourable Anglo-Tibetan agreement.

Shortly after his return, in 1907, Ugyen Wangchuck was appointed hereditary ruler of Bhutan with the title Druk Gyalpo, precious ruler of the Dragon people. The British diplomat, Sir Claude White, a great friend of the Bhutanese, was invited to the coronation at the royal winter residence at Punakha. The regime was fully recognized by the British, and Ugyen was accorded the British title of Sir. Despite all this bonhomie, the new sovereign kept all foreign influence out of the country, and there was no permanent British resident in Bhutan. All mutual diplomatic contact went through the British representative in Sikkim (who also dealt with Nepal). In 1910, however, the Treaty of Punakha was concluded between the two countries.

In 1926, Ugyen, who had proved to be a strong and capable leader, was succeeded by his son Jigme Wangchuck, who reigned until his death in 1952. During this period, great strides were taken in the unification and consolidation of the identity of Bhutan. Towards the end of Jigme Wangchuck's reign, the British left India to independence, and new ties and treaties were taken up with the independent Indian government, strengthening existing links and providing for a much greater element of aid to Bhutan. But for all this, Bhutan remained an isolated and almost feudal society. It was during the reign of Jigme Dorji Wangchuck (1952–72) that the greatest changes took place as Bhutan moved towards its place in the modern world.

8. Bhutan Today

Since 1950, events have moved rapidly in this corner of Asia, and it has proved impossible for Bhutan to ignore the changes taking place around it, even if it had wanted to. The British had departed from India, and soon afterwards, from 1950 onwards, the Chinese began to enter Tibet in force and subsequently communication and trade with Bhutan's main trading partner were almost totally severed. In 1951, Nepal's period of isolation under the Ranas ended, as we have already seen, and the country entered a new phase of open international relations under the reinstated monarchy.

In 1952, Jigme Dorji Wangchuck succeeded to the throne as the third Druk Gyalpo, and a new era began for Bhutan. In 1953, the new king voluntarily requested that the National Assembly, to be known as the Tshogdu, should be reconvened, and he abandoned his right of veto, a brave gesture when there was no real political need for him to do so. The Tshogdu, which meets now in the new Tashichhodzong in Thimpu, is made up of about 150 representatives of which about one hundred are elected by the people (serving in three-year terms), ten from the monastic order, and the remainder are chosen by the king from amongst the government posts. The system apparently works well, with lively and open discussion on most topics, and secret ballots on major issues.

In 1956, serfdom was abolished officially, though it had declined considerably anyway, and various improvements were made in the system of land tenure. The Royal Advisory Council was established in 1965 and a Council of Ministers was set up in 1968. At the same time, the king gave the power to the Assembly to force any king who might act against the interests of the country to abdicate. After years of thought and preliminary effort, the first Five Year Plan was launched in 1961, and Bhutan is now into its fifth such plan. It would not be true to say that the economy had been totally transformed in this period – rather it has advanced on some fronts and remained static on others, in a serious attempt to balance the old and the new. Unlike Nepal, which broadly speaking has sought to adopt as much as possible of the western world, constrained only by its physical and social limitations, Bhutan has recognized the advantages of what it already has – and the disadvantages of some of what it might get – and a strong policy has been adopted of integrating the two approaches, even where financial considerations would have dictated otherwise. Being, perhaps, one of the last countries in the world to embark on a development programme, Bhutan has had the advantage of being able to see the pitfalls that can arise (not that this has prevented other developing countries from falling into them), and the motto throughout has been to tread with caution, testing and evaluating as progress is made.

Industrialization of Bhutan has not proved an easy matter. Early priorities involved the production of commodities which Bhutan itself needed – hydro-electric projects, a cement factory at Samchi, etc. – or on the organization of small-scale industries for which Bhutan possessed the skills anyway. There has been, however, a considerable shortage of managerial, technical and entrepreneurial skills, and in some cases even a shortage of labour, for in Bhutan there is under-employment in contrast to the situation in most countries of the world. At the same time, there have been transport and communication difficulties, a shortage of power, a small home market, a lack of finance and so on, so all aspects have had to develop on an equal front.

India, who is on very friendly terms with Bhutan and who also has a particular desire to influence the progress of the country, has provided much of the money, manpower, and technical expertise for Bhutan's industrialization. Roads, factories and hydro-electric power stations have been built almost entirely through Indian effort, and considerable finance has been provided to allow the government to make contributions to industry and set up industrial estates at Phuntsholing, Gaylegphug and Samdrup Jongkhar. Other countries have played a markedly subordinate role, and indeed India sees Bhutan very much as its own responsibility, disgusted at Nepal's attitude in seeking aid from all comers. The others, including Australia, Britain, Switzerland and the United States of America have tended to concentrate on small specific projects – a canning factory, cheese production, aspects of education, and so on – rather than the broad coverage provided by India.

Bhutan's mineral wealth has been systematically surveyed, from the surface at least, since the 1960s, and a wealth of resources has been revealed – coal, dolomite, lead, marble, zinc and copper, to name a few – though few have been exploited and many may prove difficult of extraction. At present, coal is mined, and dolomite and limestone are quarried, all mainly for local use.

Agriculture has been greatly strengthened as an industry. With its small population, good climate, and wide altitude range, Bhutan is favourably placed to produce a very wide variety of crops, and indeed the country has always been more or less self-sufficient in food. However, the agriculture has been at a relatively primitive level, and the need has been felt for the improvement of methods and varieties, the introduction of new crops, and the creation of cash crops intended primarily for export. To this end, various agricultural research stations and demonstration programmes have been set up, and agricultural courses have been established. The country's largest research station is at Bhur, in the south, comprising 225 acres, and this combines the trial and production of all forms of crops with the education of students. Veterinary and animal breeding centres have been set up elsewhere.

One particular noticeable feature of this improvement programme has been the establishment of fruit orchards. The way into Thimpu is lined with apple orchards, and elsewhere in the midland areas, plums, peaches, apricots and other temperate top fruits are grown. In the lowlands, citrus fruits, bananas, mangoes and guavas are now grown commercially, and much of the produce is bottled, canned or turned into delicious juice at factories within the country. Some 70 per cent of the country is covered with forest (compare this with less than 10 per cent for the least forested countries in Europe) comprising a great variety of trees and forest types. This resource has now been adequately mapped, and controlled exploitation is beginning. There is every sign that Bhutan intends to do this sensibly and wisely. Desho Dorji, in charge of forests at the time, is quoted as saying 'We must not squander this, our greatest resource, and, although the financiers do not always agree with me, I feel we have a duty to our children to replant every hectare of woodland that we cut'. One can only hope that such a wise policy continues to prevail, having seen the disasters that follow mass deforestation elsewhere in the Himalayas.

Road building is proceeding apace, largely under the auspices of the Indian Border Roads Organization. Until 1960, there were no roads in the country, and the wheel itself was virtually absent. In 1960, the highway from Phuntsholing to Thimpu and Paro was started, and since then all the main towns and strategic places have been connected by roads, though they are by no means always easy roads.

Air travel has lagged behind, largely because of the shortage of space for runways, and the physical difficulties of flying, though we can expect more of a network of STOL airstrips to develop in a similar fashion to Nepal. There is a commercial air service from Paro to Calcutta, and in 1981 the Bhutanese airline Druk Air officially began an international service.

Other communications date from post-1960 also. In 1962, a postal service was initiated, and this now covers most parts of the country. There is also a reasonable phone network, and some international telecommunication facilities.

To keep pace with all this planned development, a programme of education has been essential. Until modern times, all education was in the hands of the monasteries, and a few secular schools, but there are now some 140 schools run by the government. All education is completely free, right through to further education and all books, equipment and transport are provided. Considering that Bhutan is one of the few countries in the world which does not levy direct taxes, the financing of such a scheme is no easy matter. The medium of education is generally English, but Dzongkha is a compulsory subject. The curricula always include traditional arts and crafts, and many basic skills, and they are specifically intended to prevent an over-educated élite from developing, in the sense that all is geared towards the needs of the country. Teacher training is now available, and an increasing number of teachers are trained in Bhutan, while there are plans to open a university – the Ugyen Wangchuck University – within the next few years. Many Bhutanese students receive further education abroad in India, Japan, Australia, Britain, the United States of America and elsewhere under various fellowship plans. Students returning from such courses (and they almost invariably do return) are given short courses at home to re-familarize them with Bhutan's real needs, and then they are required to work in rural areas for periods of six months or more, which generally helps them to lose their more extravagant ideas! At the same time, opportunities for monastic education continue to be provided, though a much smaller proportion of the population is entering the monkhood.

Perhaps the most significant of Bhutan's new enterprises, and the one which will ultimately be its highest foreign currency earner, if it isn't already, is tourism. Again, Bhutan is treading the path very gently, despite the potential rapid returns. There are too many examples of the disadvantages of tourism close at hand for the Bhutanese to wish to rush matters. Bhutan has only really become open to tourists in any significant numbers since 1974, and it now has a capacity for 10,000 visitors a year. In practice, the number of visitors is much lower, largely because of seasonal peaks and troughs. All tourism is organized through the National Tourism Promotion and Bhutan Travel Agency, and is virtually confined to group travellers. It is also expensive at 130 dollars per day, and limited to certain sites and routes. There is also a general tendency, we have found, to expect visitors to want to see only the great sights, and not to want to visit the markets, talk to the people, or go behind the scenes. Even more compellingly than in other countries, the best way to see and know the country is to go trekking (see Chapter 9). The Bhutanese are, however, gradually realizing that people do want more than just a 'clinical' tour, and realizing also that no aspect of Bhutanese life need be hidden. Most travellers to the Himalayas want something other than that they can find at home.

Bhutanese foreign relations have broadened considerably since the country came out of its shell. In 1962, Bhutan became a member of the Colombo Plan for co-operative economic development in South and South-East Asia. In 1968, Bhutan sent her first observers to the United Nations, while in 1969 she joined the Universal Postal Union (and now incidentally produces a great range of unusual and attractive stamps, which are also considerable foreign currency earners). With Indian and Nepalese sponsorship, Bhutan was elected to become a member of the UN by unanimous decision of the General Assembly, and the permanent Mission of the Kingdom of Bhutan to the UN was opened in New York. When Bangladesh became independent, in December 1971, Bhutan was one of the first countries to recognize her diplomatically, and diplomatic representatives were exchanged shortly afterwards. In the same year, a Royal Bhutan Mission was opened in New Delhi, later upgraded to an Embassy in 1978. In 1973, Bhutan became a member of the non-aligned group, and His Majesty Jigme Singye Wangchuck (the present king) attended the summit conference of the non-aligned movement in 1976 at Colombo.

Despite heavy reliance on her neighbours, especially India,

Bhutan's foreign policy is essentially one of peace, friendship and non-alignment. The future for Bhutan looks bright, and one can do no better than quote the king of Bhutan, writing in 1979, as a way of understanding Bhutan's way ahead: 'Our aim . . . has been and continues to be threefold. First we are committed politically to a strong and loyal sense of nationhood, to ensuring the peace and security of our citizens, and the sovereign territorial integrity of our land.

Secondly, our goal is to achieve economic self-reliance, and the capacity to begin and complete any project we undertake. At the same time, we have been concerned to preserve the ancient religious and cultural heritage that has for so many centuries strengthened and enriched our lives. That we have been able, to date, to achieve this essential balance between the values of the past and the innovations of the present is extremely encouraging.'

9. Places to Visit in Bhutan

We have probably already said enough to indicate that Bhutan has a lot to offer the visitor. This chapter is designed to highlight some of the specific places and activities that one could see on a visit. At the time of writing, the east of the country is closed to visitors, and only limited routes are available for trekking elsewhere, so we have concentrated on those places that are accessible.

General

There are certain aspects of Bhutanese life that are worth seeking out to see. Archery is the national sport, and it is played in great high spirits and with considerable skill, with the participants always wearing national dress. Archery matches take place frequently, for numerous reasons, and they are well worth seeking out. Sunday is the best day.

Festivals are numerous and always colourful. Many of them are spectacular, and include dancing and rituals dating back hundreds of years, sometimes to the days before Buddhism. Like Nepalese festivals, they are not held according to our calendar, but according to the Bhutanese lunar calendar which is based on the Chinese and Tibetan model. Thus, one cannot usefully predict the dates of festivals. They occur frequently, though, especially in spring and autumn, and are normally based at dzongs or monasteries. If you have a flexible itinerary, it is well worth finding out what is going on in the vicinity.

Markets, often held on a Sunday, are an endless source of delight, not to mention photographs. These remain as they have always been, with basic commodities bartered for or bought and sold, and a few more modern items here and there. The colour and activity, set against the backdrop of Bhutanese scenery, is a remarkable sight.

Even in the sunday street market in Thimpu, it is refreshing to see how little is aimed at the tourist, and one is never pestered. Some of the hand-woven cloths on sale here are really beautiful, though hardly cheap.

Phuntsholing

Phuntsholing is the main entry point for land travellers to Bhutan, on the edge of the Indian plains. It is not a particularly attractive town, more Indian than Bhutanese in character, though the border gateway is impressive. There is an excellent hotel, up a long track, on the hills overlooking Phuntsholing, with beautiful sunset views and fine forest all around. We've frequently seen deer in the forests, and there are numerous birds also. It is a good centre for seeing lowland Bhutan, if you are interested in fishing, or natural history, but access is generally difficult.

Thimpu

If driving from Phuntsholing to Thimpu, there is a high pass along the way with superb views of both India and Bhutan. Thimpu itself is, in some ways, disappointing if one is familiar with Kathmandu or Darjeeling. It is much smaller, with a population of only about 20,000, and many of the buildings have been built, of modern materials, in the last few years. It therefore has neither the architectural spectacle nor the exciting bustle of Kathmandu, nor are there particularly good views of the mountains, but for all that it has a charm of its own and some fine buildings. Since 1955 it has been the nation's permanent capital, and it lies at 7500 feet, an ideal altitude for Bhutan. The most obvious and spectacular of its buildings is the Tashichhodzong, built a few years ago to house the nation's government. The present building is a rebuilt version of a dzong that was erected here by Ngawang Namgyal in 1641, and it retains many of the features of the old dzong. It is now an impressive sight, and altogether it houses all the government departments and ministries, the throne room of the king, the National Assembly chambers, and the nation's largest monastery with 2000 monks and a religious administrative centre! The coronation of the present king was held here in 1974. The buildings, especially the temples, hold many fine carvings and works of art.

A few miles downstream from Thimpu, at the mouth of the valley, lies the Simtokha Dzong, the oldest dzong in Bhutan. It was built in

1627 by Namgyal, as the first of his chain of dzongs, and it still stands in good condition. It was also the country's first centre of religious education and even now houses a school for monastic studies. The Jigme Dorji Wangchuck memorial chorten, although uninspiring architecturally, is beautiful inside with carvings and paintings depicting numerous deities in all their aspects.

On a high hill to the west of Thimpu, at about 10,000 feet, lies the Phajoding monastery with superb views of the mountains and of the town and valley below. Several of the passes around the valley provide spectacular views of the Himalayas along the northern border and back into midland Bhutan.

The royal family's residence near Thimpu, at Dechencholing, is a beautiful example of Bhutanese architecture, set amongst lawns and ponds.

Punakha Valley

Punakha is just close enough to Thimpu to make a long day trip worthwhile, taking the new road over the 10,000 foot Dochu La pass. The pass is reached in about an hour from Thimpu, and the views to the north especially are superb, with a great line of snow peaks clearly visible. The Punakha valley lies way below, down such a long, steep drop that it hardly seems possible that the road can continue. The drive down goes through alpine forests at first, but gradually the countryside becomes noticeably drier and hotter (Punakha lies in a rain shadow, and is also at a much lower altitude than other midland valleys, so its climate is warm and sheltered) as you descend. Despite the excellent climate, and the possibility of growing an endless variety of crops, the population density of the valley is remarkably low, and there are few houses or villas. The highlight of the valley is the ancient fortress-like Punakha Dzong, built in 1637, and once the capital of Bhutan. It is imposingly situated at the confluence of the Pho Chu and the Mo Chu, and it has been damaged many times by spring or summer floods from one or other of these rivers.

Until very recently, Punakha remained the winter capital of Bhutan (there is now only one capital – Thimpu), and it is still the winter quarters of the Head Abbot (Je Khempo), and his monks who transfer every year from Thimpu. It is also the place where Jigme Dorji Wangchuck convened the first National Assembly (Tshogdu) in 1952, and the remains of the first Shabdung, Ngawang Namgyal, are buried there.

The Paro Valley

The Paro valley has the reputation of being the most beautiful of Bhutan's main valleys, and the reputation is justly deserved. It is possible to trek from Thimpu to Paro (see below, under *Trekking*), but the normal method of approach is by road. It is also the site of Bhutan's largest airstrip, capable of handling moderate-sized planes such as Fokkers, and the only international airstrip in Bhutan. Paro itself is only a small village, with Paro Dzong as its centrepoint, and very few shops and houses compared to Thimpu. There are few souvenirs to speak of, other than what local people would buy anyway, very few tourists, and no hassles from anybody. Many people speak English, and there are at present large numbers of Nepalese there working on various projects including the construction of the hotel, a three-storeyed affair. Like Punakha, the population density is low, and wildlife abounds undisturbed. Choughs are everywhere, and the rare ibisbill nests on the shingle by the river.

The dominant feature of Paro itself is undoubtedly the Paro Dzong, set just above the glacial Paro Chu. It is a particularly historic and important dzong that has played a part in Bhutan's history since its first construction, and the site itself has an even longer history. It is known that Padma Sambhava himself built a temple here in the ninth century, and this was used for the site of the construction of an imposing, fortress-like, five-storey dzong by Ngawang Namgyal in 1646. For two and a half centuries, this stone-built dzong served as a key defence post against invasions from the north, until finally the 'Rinpung' Dzong was burnt down in 1907, taking all its remarkable religious treasures with it, except one. The one item saved was an enormous and beautiful Thangka (wall-hanging) known as the Thongdel. It is about 100 by 150 feet in size, depicting Padma Sambhava (Guru Rimpoche) the bringer of Buddhism to Bhutan, flanked by two consorts. On New Year's Day the Thangka is brought out, unrolled, and hung on a wall of the monastery for a few hours, while dancing and pageants take place in front of it. When it is rolled up again, a protective cloth is placed over each image by the monks.

The present monastery was built, to the traditional pattern, almost immediately afterwards, by Penlop (governor) Dawa Penjor, and it now houses a collection of both ancient and modern religious dress and artefacts. Above the dzong stands the largest of the original watchtowers (the Ta Dzong), which has been beautifully restored and now houses the national museum of Bhutan, in a particularly apt and beautiful site. The other watchtowers are now ruined. Across an ancient bridge lies the Ugyen Pelri palace, a royal residence said to have been built on the lines of the heavenly abode of the first Shabdung. Before the new Tashichhodzong was built, the Paro Dzong was the seat of the National Assembly.

A few miles to the north, close to the airstrip, lies the country's oldest temple, the Kyichu Lakhang, vying for the honour with another temple in Bumthang. Parts of the temple date from the seventh or eighth century, and precious relics dating back to the earliest days of Buddhism in Bhutan are preserved there. There are also a series of white chortens depicting the coming of some of the earliest Buddhist missionaries, sent by that great Buddhist zealot, King Tsongtsangampo of Tibet. The central temple was built much later, in 1830, and the golden roof was added later.

A few miles up the valley lies one of the most intriguing and romantic of the valley's dzongs, the Drukgyel Dzong, now in ruins after a fire in 1954. It is imposingly situated on a hill, with views away to Chomolhari, and it can be approached only from one side, protected by three tall towers. There is a fascinating turreted passageway, still in good condition, which was designed to ensure a supply of water even in times of siege. The dzong was built, by Namgyal of course, to commemorate an early victory over the Tibetans, and the name means 'Victorious Dragon Dzong'. Away through the woods, only approachable by narrow paths, is the solitary Hadi Gompa, rarely visited except by the most ardent of pilgrims.

The highspot of the Paro valley, and one of the few features of Bhutan known to the outside world, is the incredible Taktsang monastery, the 'Tiger's Nest'. It is built, clinging like a limpet on a sheer 3000 foot cliff face, approachable only by the narrowest of paths. Its origins lie back in the eighth century, when Padma Sambhava brought Buddhism to the country, and meditated here on his way through. A simple temple was built then surrounded by monks' caves and hermitages, but gradually the complex has been added to, and much of the present building is of seventeenth-century origin. One can ride up most of the way on horseback – a somewhat unnerving experience – though the last section has to be walked, preferably without looking down! The whole thing – temples, chapels and residences – is built and maintained entirely without nails, in the traditional Bhutanese style. It is an extraordinary and dramatic place, not to be missed, even if you do not feel like going all the way up.

Higher still than Taktsang, on top of the ridge, is the relatively new (300 year old) Sangtog Peri monastery with a commanding position high up above the Paro valley. Elsewhere in the valley, there are other hermitages and small temples, some built into the cliffs, and the houses here are amongst the finest examples of domestic Bhutanese architecture – perfectly maintained whitewashed gems amongst the bright green fields.

Wangdiphodrang

The furthest east that most travellers go is to the dzong at Wangdiphodrang, at the junction of the Mo Chu and Tang Chu rivers. Not far away is a yak research station, and a military camp close to the village. Few tourists reach Wangdiphodrang.

The Eastern Towns

There are a number of centres towards the east of the country that are still inaccessible to the visitor, and these include Tongsa, Bumthang, Tashigang and Mongar Dzong. Tongsa is famous for its dzong, from which Ugyen Wangchuck governed Tongsa as its Penlop, before being crowned as the first of the hereditary monarchs at the beginning of this century. His successor as king continued to rule the country from here, and even the present king holds the formal post of Penlop of Tongsa. The dzong itself was constructed by Ngawang Namgyal in 1648, and has been added to by successive residents, so that it is now a great sprawling many-levelled structure tumbling down the hillside. There are now over twenty temples within the complex, each recognizable by the golden symbols that surmount the roof over the altar.

Bumthang, further east, is becoming a significant centre, with canning and bottling industries, and research and teaching facilities. It is also redolent with history and legend, particularly associated with Padma Sambhava, but also with the later Buddhist teacher and saint, Pemalingpa. It was at Bumthang that Padma Sambhava cured the then ruler, an Indian called Sindhu Raja, of a serious disease. Temples and shrines were erected in his honour, and many of the old shrines and buildings have some association with this man. But the legend of Pemalingpa is even stranger. Pemalingpa was born as a blacksmith in the fifteenth century, and apart from his small stature, seemed quite normal until he was twenty-seven. Then he met a hermit who gave him a roll of paper, and, though he couldn't read, he understood that it conveyed the message, 'go to the Burning Lake'. This he did, and on arriving there with little idea of what to do, he stared down into the lake. Suddenly he was carried down and down to a temple at the bottom, where he met an old woman who gave him a casket which she said was from Guru Rimpoche (Padma Sambhava). He returned to the surface, realizing that he was probably a reincarnation of Guru Rimpoche, and that it was incumbent on him to teach the words of Buddha. But as he knew nothing of religion, he felt completely at a loss, so he spent the night in the open, away from the village. During the night he miraculously acquired knowledge of all the religions of the world, and the following morning he began to teach. He went on to become one of Bhutan's most famous religious teachers, revered to this day.

The Manas Sanctuary

In the lowlands adjacent to Assam, in southeast Bhutan, the Manas Game Sanctuary lies astride the Manas river. It consists of some 60 square miles of low-lying alluvial jungle and grassland, with some of the densest populations of wildlife in the sub-continent. It is comparable physically with Chitwan, but it is richer, with endemic species such as the Golden langur, and less disturbed. Like Chitwan, there are rhinos, tigers, leopards, chital, Pigmy hog, crocodiles, and even wild elephants, all in remarkable abundance, with a profuse bird life. At present, it is not really accessible to the normal visitor, though there are hopes that it will open again in the near future.

Trekking in Bhutan

At present, opportunities for trekking are limited, though more than adequate for the once-in-a-lifetime visitor to Bhutan. The three treks permitted at present are the Chili La, between Paro and Ha; the Paro-Thimpu trek, and the Chomolhari Base Camp trek. There are hopes that more treks in the highland Lunana region will soon be permitted.

Trekking in Bhutan is different in many ways to trekking in Nepal. First, there are far, far, less people, both resident and visitor and one may travel all day hardly meeting anyone. Secondly, facilities are not geared towards trekkers; thirdly, except in special circum-stances, it is not possible to travel alone – you have to travel in a group. And finally, information – books, maps and verbal information – is very difficult to come by, and many visitors find this frustrating. But if you can accept the lack of facilities, Bhutan is a dream come true for the walker, with fabulous, totally unspoilt scenery and natural history, gently overlaid by the remarkable and beautiful Bhutanese culture.

The Chili La trek starts at Paro. Dense forest is soon reached (excellent for views of pheasants), and then the ridge. As you gain height, increasingly panoramic views of the mountains open out towards Chomolhari, Kangphu Kang and Kula Kangri up on the northern border. The high pass at Kalai La is a sacred place with many prayer flags, and the coffins or bones of children who have died, put here for the vultures and ravens (the method of disposing of the dead varies, but it is quite common practice to wire down a corpse on a high point, and let the spirit be released as the flesh is eaten away). By about day four, one spends all the time amongst high yak pastures, well covered with flowers in spring, and views as far afield as Kanchenjunga on a clear day. The Sage La is another important burial area. Gradually the trail descends into the deciduous forest and onto the drier slopes above the Paro valley. Although a short trek, a tremendous range of conditions are encountered, an enormous amount of wildlife seen, and some fabulous mountain views experienced. We have been with other trekkers who have walked widely elsewhere in the Himalayas, and all seem to agree that high altitude Bhutan takes a lot of beating.

The Paro-Thimpu trek is short and relatively easy, comparable perhaps to the Helambu trek in Nepal. It provides a useful introduction to trekking in Bhutan, and also an opportunity to sample the real rural Bhutan. There are also some fine ridge views, dense forests, and good bird life.

The Chomolhari Base Camp trek is undoubtedly the hardest trek currently available. It is not particularly long, but it involves four high passes and a good deal of high altitude work. Chomolhari itself (24,000 feet) is one of the few climbed Bhutanese peaks, scaled by an Indo-Bhutanese team in 1970, and the Base Camp dates from this expedition. The trek starts, by road, from Thimpu, and walking starts at Dodina, about an hour's drive away. Base Camp is reached in four to five days, and the trek returns via Drukgyel Dzong to Paro, taking eight to nine days in all. The higher reaches of this trek have a very Tibetan or Central Asian feel, and it is not uncommon for instance to see large numbers of Blue sheep. Bear are often seen, and several trekkers have told us of 'Big Cats' they have seen at very high altitudes (possibly the very rare Snow leopard, or its lowland cousin straying out of the forest zone). There is certainly no other readily available trek quite like it anywhere else.

10. Sikkim

Sikkim has had a chequered history, culminating after periods as a British protectorate, then an Indian protectorate with its annexation as the twenty-second state of the Republic of India in 1975. It is no longer a Himalayan kingdom, more of a remote and partly Buddhist corner of India, gradually succumbing to Indian influence and values.

Nevertheless, it retains its old country boundaries as a state, and away from the main routes and centres the old Sikkim is very evident, with its monasteries, peaceful villages and predominantly Buddhist culture. It is no less mountainous than its two Himalayan neighbours, with a host of high peaks culminating in the third highest peak in the world, Kanchenjunga (28,208 feet high) on the borders with Nepal. In fact, it is more consistently mountainous with virtually no lowland zone, and very little flat land at all.

With an area of only 2818 square miles, Sikkim was for a long time the smallest country in Central Asia, and throughout history it has fought constant battles to retain its identity and borders. Its last recorded population size as an independent kingdom was 200,000 people, distributed mainly through the south, west and centre of the country. The capital, Gangtok, lies in the southwest.

Sikkim's climate is essentially very similar to the adjacent parts of its neighbours, with a rainy season in the summer monsoon. The rainfall at Gangtok is about 140 inches per year, wetter than both Kathmandu and Thimpu, and generally Sikkim has the lush feel of a country with high rainfall. The same seasonal pattern prevails (see Chapter 2), and the same advice to travellers applies. Sikkim's natural history, considering the country's small size and absence of a Terai zone, is perhaps even more remarkable than that of its neighbours. Some 700 bird species have been recorded, including thirty-two not found in Nepal; there are over 4000 species of flowering plants, including at least forty rhododendrons and over 450 orchids. There are also over 600 species of butterfly recorded. In general, the flora and fauna is much better known than that of Bhutan, deriving from the freer access given to the British in India, dating from the time of Hooker's *Himalayan Journals*, and other great naturalist-travellers.

The indigenous people of Sikkim are known as the Lepchas. They have no written or oral tradition of migration, and there are no records of such, so it is probable that they are an original or very long established people. They speak a Tibeto-Burman language with a script devised in the eighteenth century by King Chagdor Namgyal. Their religion is Buddhism, though like many Nepalese and Bhutanese, their original religion was Bonism, and even today their Buddhism contains elements of the old religion. Other very long established and possibly indigenous tribes include the Magars (as in Nepal) and the Tsongs, both of Mongolian type and both renowned warriors.

From about the thirteenth century onwards, Tibetan-speaking Bhutias entered the country from the Kham area of Tibet. They were led by a prince of the Namgyal dynasty, from whom the last Chogyal (hereditary king) of Sikkim was descended. Most of these Bhutias settled in the midland valleys to become farmers, and there has been considerable mixing with the Lepchas.

In the mid-nineteenth century, there was a series of major immigrations, mainly from north and east Nepal. The Newars came first, followed by Gurungs, Tamangs, Rais and Sherpas, many of whom settled at higher altitudes. They brought with them the techniques of terracing, so familiar in Nepal, which were put into use wherever land was short. These migrations were followed by lowland Nepalis, Chetris in particular, who brought Hinduism with them. This mixture of Nepalese races brought a typically Nepalese mixture of Buddhism and Hinduism with it, and this amalgamation has been absorbed into the Sikkimese religious way of life.

In the mid-eighteenth century a series of territorial wars were fought with Bhutan over Bhutan's expansionist ideas. Later in the century there were a series of wars with Nepal, started of course by Prithwi Narayan Shah, which lasted well into the nineteenth century. Eventually the Nepalese came to occupy much of western Sikkim, though they relinquished part in 1793, and the remaining lower-lying areas in 1816. Then in 1839, the British East India Company obtained Darjeeling from Sikkim for use as a health resort

Sikkim

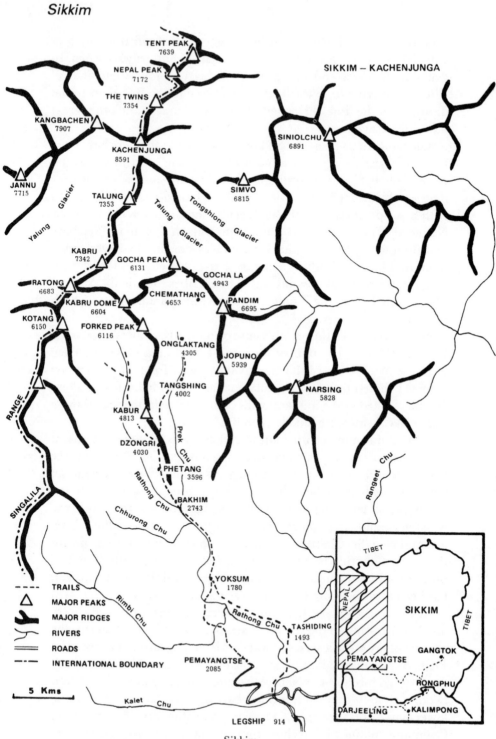

TENT PEAK
7639

NEPAL PEAK
7172

THE TWINS
7354

KANGBACHEN
7907

KACHENJUNGA
8591

JANNU
7715

TALUNG
7353

Yalung

Glacier

Talung Glacier

Tongshiong Glacier

SIKKIM — KACHENJUNGA

SINIOLCHU
6891

SIMVO
6815

KABRU
7342

GOCHA PEAK
6131

GOCHA LA
4943

RATONG
6683

CHEMATHANG
4653

PANDIM
6695

KABRU DOME
6604

KOTANG
6150

FORKED PEAK
6116

ONGLAKTANG
4305

JOPUNO
5939

NARSING
5828

TANGSHING
4002

RANGE

KABUR
4813

Prek Chu

DZONGRI
4030

SINGALILA

PHETANG
3596

Rathong Chu

BAKHIM
2743

Ranget Chu

Chhurong Chu

YOKSUM
1780

Rimbi Chu

TRAILS

MAJOR PEAKS

MAJOR RIDGES

RIVERS

ROADS

INTERNATIONAL BOUNDARY

Rathong Chu

TASHIDING
1493

5 Kms

PEMAYANGTSE
2085

Kalet Chu

LEGSHIP 914

Sikkim

TIBET

NEPAL

SIKKIM

GANGTOK

PEMAYANGTSE

TIBET

RONGPHU

DARJEELING

KALIMPONG

and hill station. As the British became established, they sought to bring Sikkim within their sphere of influence. They annexed the lowland areas, which led to various uprisings in protest. The British eventually defeated the Sikkimese, and this led to the signing of an Anglo-Sikkimese treaty in 1861. This recognized Sikkim's sovereignty, and established her as a buffer state, while granting various concessions to the British, including the right to build a road through to Tibet.

In 1890, the Tibetans mounted a series of incursions across the northern border into Sikkim. At an Anglo-Chinese convention, the Chinese recognized Britain's special relationship with Sikkim, and a formal boundary was established. Shortly afterwards, a British political officer was assigned to assist the Chogyal. After Indian independence, Sikkim signed a treaty with the new government in India. Sikkim was deemed to be an Indian protectorate, and an Indian representative took up residence in Gangtok. This marked the beginning of a period of internal strife, as Sikkim's infant political parties jostled for power and in disagreement over their attitude to India. Finally, after a long, difficult period, Sikkim's independent status was abolished and she entered India as the twenty-second state. The reigning Chogyal (Palden Thondup Namgyal, a descendant of the thirteenth-century immigrant prince) was deposed, and Sikkim began to be governed by India.

Travel around Sikkim is, at present, severely limited for non-Indian nationals. It is a politically sensitive area, especially in the north and east, and access to many areas is closed despite the remarkably good road network.

Regrettably, Gangtok is a severe disappointment. It is a small town of 15,000 to 20,000 people set in a valley at 5600 feet, but it lacks almost anything of architectural merit or particular beauty. There are a few fine buildings and temples, but much of the town is a sprawl of relatively new building. It is, however, the state capital, and is frequently visited for administrative reasons if nothing else, though it is possible to avoid it if you prefer.

Although outside the present-day borders of the state, Darjeeling has to be mentioned in any account of Sikkim. Apart from being the main road gateway, it retains many of its old links with Sikkim, and even with Tibet by virtue of the retired Tibetan traders there, and it is one of the most relaxing and attractive towns in the Himalayas. The architecture is an intriguing blend of British Raj and Sikkimese, it is full of fascinating characters and activity, and everywhere there are tea gardens and breathtaking views of Kanchenjunga. Kalimpong, some fifteen miles to the east, is almost as nice, though smaller and quieter.

Pemayengtse is a small village north of Gyalzing with a beautiful monastery, one of the oldest in Sikkim, centre of the Nyingmapa sect of Buddhism. The carvings and wall-hangings are remarkably fine. The village is also the normal starting point for the only trek allowed to visitors (see below). There is a lodge there, with fabulous mountain views, though accommodation is severely limited and needs to be booked.

There is only one trek that is at present normally open to visitors, though many other areas of the country would be fascinating for trekking. Trekking in Sikkim, as in Bhutan, is in its infancy, and facilities are minimal such that camping equipment is essential. At present it is virtually impossible to trek alone. The permitted trek is the Dzongri ridge trek towards Kanchenjunga. Although it is not a long trek, and it is the only one, it makes up for all this by its quality. There are superb views throughout with the great bulk of Kanchenjunga dominating the whole walk. The trek takes place in an area that is virtually without roads and with no main centres, and the original Buddhist way of life prevails in a calm remoteness. Like Bhutan, the population densities are much lower than in most of Nepal, and this is reflected in the greater amount of forest, the more abundant and more visible wildlife, and in the overall peacefulness. There are also, of course, few other trekkers. Without really trying, we recorded over 110 species of birds in one ten-day midwinter trek.

The highpoint of the trek is the few days spent around the stone hut at Dzongri (recently rebuilt after collapsing under the weight of snow). From here, one can climb in various directions, including several minor peaks accessible within the day, and the views of mountains and glaciers are superb. It is possible to spend days here at 13,000 feet without meeting a soul. In spring, the high altitude flowers are abundant, much better than further west, though there is always more snow lying in Sikkim (because it snows more heavily), so the season tends to be later. The return, through Bakhim and Yoksum, involves some fine ridge walking, several hot springs, and a beautiful monastery at Tashiding. As far as we are concerned, this is the real Sikkim dating from the days as a kingdom, greatly preferable to the modern Indian Sikkim close by.

Glossary

Many Nepalese, Tibetan and other words appear frequently on maps and in books about this region, and the commonest of these are listed here. It should be borne in mind that the Nepali or Tibetan equivalent is transliterated from a different script (except in the case of Sherpa words, which have no written equivalent), so spellings may vary considerably, depending on the interpretation of individual authors or cartographers.

Native word	English equivalent
Bhatt	Boiled rice
Chang	Local beer, brewed from various sources
Chauthara	Porter's resting place, where the load can be placed
Chiso	Cold
Chiya (Chia)	Tea
Chomolungma	Everest
Chuba	Long Tibetan robe
Daal (Dhal)	Lentils, usually cooked
Doko	Large conical carrying basket, carried on the back
Dorje	Symbolic lightning bolt
Dudh	Milk
Degupuja	Regular daily worship of household deities
Gaida	Indian one-horned rhinoceros
Garbh	The base of a stupa, representing Buddha's body
Ghore	Horse
Gompa	Monastery
Goth	Summer grazing huts
Haimika	The square tower of a stupa
Himal	Mountain range
Khola, Kosi	Rivers of different sizes
Kund	Lake

Glossary

Lekh	Hill or mountain range
Nadi	Small river
Namaste	Universal greeting in Nepal, meaning hello, welcome, and even goodbye
Pahad	Mountain
Pani	Water
Parbat	Mountain
Pais, Paisa	Money, literally hundredths of a rupee
Pathi	Measure of liquid, about 1 gill
Pokhari	Lakes
Pul	Bridge (cf. *Phul* or *Ful* = eggs)
Rakhshi	Local clear spirit, usually from rice
Sagarmatha	Everest
Sati	Where the wife throws herself on the funeral pyre of her dead husband
Shikhara	A particular form of temple, originating in India
Stupa	Buddhist religious monument in the form of Buddha
Tal	Lake
Thole	Ward (of a town), street
Thankas	Tibetan religious wall scrolls
Torana	Gateway to the inner sanctum of a pagoda
Tsampa	Roasted barley meal, the staple diet of many hill tribes

Bibliography

General Reading

Bernstein, J. *The Wildest Dreams of Kew: A Profile of Nepal*. New York, Simon & Schuster, 1970.

Fletcher. *The Fabulous Flemings of Kathmandu*. Dutton, 1964.

Hagen, T. *Nepal, the Kingdom in the Himalayas*. London, Robert Hale & Co., 1972.

Hillary, E. *Schoolhouse in the Clouds*. London, Penguin, 1968.

Kazami, T. *The Himalayas. A Journey to Nepal*. Bombay, Allied Publishers, 1968.

Nicolson, N. *The Himalayas. The World's Wild Places*. Time Life Books, Amsterdam, 1975.

Peissel, M. *Tiger for Breakfast*. London, Hodder, 1966.

— *Mustang. Lost Himalayan Kingdom*. Collins.

— *The Great Himalayan Passage*. London, Collins.

Rieffel, R. *Nepal Namaste*. Kathmandu, Sahayogi Prakashan, 1975.

Rose, C. *Nepal, Strategy for Survival*. University of California, 1971.

Simpson, C. *Katmandu*. Angus & Robertson, 1967.

Snellgrove, D. *Himalayan Pilgrimage*. Oxford, Cassirer, 1961.

We have also found many articles in the following journals and papers to be of considerable interest:

The Geographical Magazine
National Geographic
Himalayan Journal
Expedition
Rising Nepal (English language daily, Kathmandu)

People of Nepal

Dor Bahadur Bista. *People of Nepal*. Kathmandu, Ratna Pustak Bhandar, 1972.

Bibliography

Furer-Haimendorf, C. von. *The Sherpas of Nepal. Buddhist Highlanders.* London, John Murray, 1964.
— *Himalayan Traders.* London, John Murray, 1975.
Hagen, T. *Nepal. Kingdom of the Himalayas.* Berne, Kummerley & Frey, 1971, 2nd ed.
Shresta, D. B., Singh, C. B., and Pradhan, B. M. *Ethnic Groups of Nepal and their Ways of Living.* Pub. by the authors, Kathmandu, 1972.
Forbes, D. *Johnny Gurkha.* Vikas, 1964.

History of Nepal

Mayne, P. *Friends in High Places.* London, The Bodley Head.
Leifer, W. *Himalaya: Mountains of Destiny.* Galley Press, 1962.
Rose, C. *Nepal, Strategy for Survival.* University of California, 1971.
Thapa, N. B. *A Short History of Nepal.* Kathmandu, Ratna Pustak Bhandar, 1973.
Nepal and the Gurkhas. HMSO, London, Ministry of Defence, 1965.

Religion and Festivals in Nepal

Anderson, M. *Festivals of Nepal.* London, George Allen & Unwin, 1971.
Bernier, R. M. *The Temples of Nepal.* Kathmandu, Voice of Nepal, 1970.
Chaudhury, R. *Temples and Legends of Nepal.* Bombay, Bharatiya Vidya Bharan, 1972.
Humphreys, C. *Buddhism.* London, Penguin, 1952.
Kansakar, P. B. *On the Hill of the Self-revealed Lord.* Kathmandu, Dreamweapon Press, 1974.
Lall, K. *Lore and Legend of Nepal.* Kathmandu, Ratna Pustak Bhandar, 1971.
Ray, A. *Art of Nepal.* Indian council for cultural relations, Delhi, 1973.
Rubel, M. *The Gods of Nepal.* Kathmandu, Bhimratna Harsharatna, 1968.
Sen, K. M. *Hinduism.* London, Penguin books, 1961.

Natural History

Ali, S. *Indian Hill Birds.* London, Oxford University Press, 1949.

Fleming, R. L., Fleming, R. L., and Bangdel, L. S. *Birds of Nepal.* Kathmandu (Box 229), the authors, 1976.

Durham University Himalayan Expedition. *Draft Langtang National Park Management Plan, and Interim Reports.* Durham University, UK, 1976 and 1977.

Gee, E. P. *The Wildlife of India.* London, Collins, 2nd ed, 1975.

Hooker, J. D. *Himalayan Journals* (Reprint of 1854 ed.). Today and Tomorrow's Printers, Delhi, 1969.

King, B., Woodcock, M. and Dickenson, E. C. *The Birds of South East Asia.* London, Collins, 1975.

Long, Tony. *Mountain Animals.* Macdonald, London, 1971.

McKinnon, J. and K. *Animals of Asia. The Ecology of the Oriental Region.* Peter Lowe, 1974.

Nicolson, N. *The Himalayas. The World's Wild Places.* Time Life Books, Amsterdam, 1975.

Prater, S. H. *The Book of Indian Mammals.* Bombay Natural History Society, 3rd edition, 1971.

Tilman, H. W. *Nepal Himalaya.* London, Cambridge University Press, 1952. See chapter by Polunin on the natural history of Langtang area.

Stainton, J. D. A. *Forests of Nepal.* London, John Murray, 1972.

In addition, there are various leaflets published by the Tourism and National Parks Departments in Nepal, covering national parks, butterflies, mammals, birds, etc.

Journals that regularly print articles of interest on Nepal include: *Journal of the Nepal Conservation Society, Journal of the Bombay Natural History Society, The Journal of the Royal Horticultural Society* (London) and subsequently *The Garden; the Bulletin of the Alpine Garden Society; Oryx.*

Trekking

Armington, S. *Exploring Nepal.* La Siesta Press, 1975.

Bezruchka, S. *A Guide to Trekking in Nepal.* Kathmandu, Sahayogi Prakashan, 1974.

Hayes, J. L. *Nepal Trekking Guidebooks.* Kathmandu, Avalok, 1975, 1976 *et seq.* A series of separate guidebooks describing treks in all the main regions of Nepal.

Prakash Raj. *Traveller's Guide to Nepal.* Lonely Planet, 1976.

Rieffel, R. *Nepal Namaste.* Kathmandu, Sahayogi Prakashan, 1975.

Ward, M. *Mountain Medicine.* Crosby, Lockwood, Staples, 1975.

Mountaineering

There are a very large number of books with accounts of climbs and expeditions, so we have simply selected a few that are 'classics' or may be of general interest.

Bonington, C. *Everest the Hard Way*. London, Hodder & Stoughton, 1976.

Hagen, T. *et al. Mount Everest: Formation, Population and Exploration of the Everest Region*. London, Oxford University Press, 1963.

Harka Gurung. *Annapurna to Dhaulgiri*. Kathmandu, Dept of Information, His Majesty's Government, 1968. A summary of mountaineering in Nepal from 1956 to 1960.

Herzog, M. *Annapurna. The first 8000 metre peak*. Jonathan Cape, 1952.

Hunt, Sir John. *The Conquest of Everest*. London, Hodder & Stoughton, 1953, and New York, Dutton & Co., 1954.

Kazami, T. *The Himalayas. A Journey to Nepal*. 'This Beautiful World', vol. 1. Allied Publishers, Bombay, 1968.

Tilman, H. W. *Nepal Himalaya*. London, Cambridge University Press, 1952.

Ullman, J. R. *Man of Everest; Tenzing*. London, Harrap, 1956.

Also numerous articles in: *Climber and Rambler, Expedition, Mountain World, The Alpine Journal*, etc.

Bhutan

Government of Bhutan. 1979. *Bhutan: Himalayan Kingdom*.

Olschak, B. C. 1971 *Bhutan: Land of Hidden Treasures*. George Allen and Unwin Ltd.

Sikkim

Normally included (inadequately) in guides to India. The recent Lonely Planet (Australia) guide is a good current example.

Hooker, J. D. *Himalayan Journals* (Reprint of 1854 ed.). Today and Tomorrow's Printers, Delhi, 1969.

Index

Index

Index